THE OLDEST SOUL

AURORA

TIFFANY FITZHENRY

ANTIQUUS

AURORA

PRIMITUS

Printed in the United States of America

First printing, 2016

All rights reserved. Published by Hierarchy Publishing, LLC

ISBN 978-1-944216-06-1 (Paperback)
ISBN 978-1-944216-07-8 (Hardcover)
ISBN 978-1-944216-08-5 (Kindle)
ISBN 978-1-944216-09-2 (Epub)

Hierarchy Publishing, LLC
1029 Peachtree Parkway, #346
Peachtree City, GA 30269
www.hierarchypublishing.com

Cover image copyright © Iko/Shutterstock.com
Cover design by Vanessa Mendozzi
Formatting by Polgarus Studio
The Oldest Soul original artwork, symbols, and interior illustrations copyright

For Denise, who helped me into the river.

AUTHOR'S NOTE

—— ❈ ——

Within the pages of this book you'll find both fact and fiction. Open your mind to see how fluid these two concepts truly are.

Note that planetary and astrological events detailed herein are accurate. All translations of different languages, defined words, symbolic meanings and interpretations are 'factual,' insofar as such things can be. Most references to real events and historic coincidences, and all mythology are also true.

As for the rest, you decide what to believe. But remember, almost everything contains another layer, every name and number you come upon, another clue.

I will be posting about each of the mysteries within this book, sorting fact from fiction, and challenging you to go deeper, not only into the world of The Oldest Soul, but in the world as we know it. Go to **TiffanyFitzhenry.com** and subscribe to my blog to learn more.

As Ralph Waldo Emerson famously said, "A mind, once stretched, can never go back to its original dimension." To stretch one's mind we must first become curious. We must be suspicious. We must wake up and remember how to think critically. The fate of the world depends on it.

"The wound is the place where the light enters you."

— Rumi

PART ONE

SULPHUR

ONE

—— ✠ ——

"The word *apocalypse*, by definition, means 'the lifting of the veil,'" my grandfather informed me out of absolutely nowhere on a walk one evening. Apparently the time had come for me to know this odd fact.

I was thirteen years old.

It was my birthday, the year was 2012, and we'd just arrived in Sulphur, Nevada for what I was told would be a very short stay.

"Maybe less than a couple of days," Cian had said. He usually tried to prepare me en route with the basic itinerary of our constant travels—at least so far as he could predict, which was always perfectly.

Except this once.

As fate would have it, we'd spend just a few hours in Sulphur, though something enormous would occur during that brief time—something that would silently set humanity on a course that there would be no turning back from—the waking of one particular soul, the soul of a young man named Thomas Greeley.

I couldn't have known it at the time, and wouldn't put the pieces together until several years later, but this single event was the trigger. It signaled the start of a grand finale of sorts. The conclusion of the story of my soul.

A story destined to change the world—by ending it forever.

"Welcome to the beginning of the end," Shamus quipped as I descended the little metal stairs of the old Winnebago we'd rented in Key West, the acrid smell of Sulphur hitting my nose like a punch. I threw my hands up to shield my eyes from the blinding light and the plume of smoky dust that billowed by—and from my brother's bizarre grin. Though it wasn't unusual for him to say strange things, meaningless things, this particular remark caught my attention. Like the putrid stench in the air, the sulfuric stink of rotting eggs, what he said was particularly off putting. Even for him.

"Why do you say *that*?" I asked.

All day I'd been sensing things were off, as if up were down and down were up, and having no real clue as to why.

This made the insecure feeling I often felt around Shamus even worse. And in keeping with the troubling pattern of the day, instead of belittling or torturing me like he usually would, Shamus just started whistling "Zip-a-Dee-Doo-Dah."

I watched as he carefully chose a nearby spot of cracked earth, set up the rusty beach chair—it came with the RV rental—plopped down in it, and turned his pasty mug toward the blazing desert sun. The searing heat that beat down on us in waves so intense it made my vision blur and ears ring was going to scorch his alabaster skin to a crisp in minutes, but he acted as if it was his personal elixir of life.

I instantly recognized that Sulphur was an uninhabitable foreign planet on which I would not survive for very long and that we'd surely driven into a vortex to a parallel universe—my brother's happiness the obvious result of possession by alien beings, though I kept that assessment to myself.

On our long journey to this mysterious destination, the farther west we traveled the noticeably more chipper Shamus became. He was even agreeable, for crying out loud. And now, as he basked in the day's final blaze of blinding solar flares like a cheerful cactus flower, he was positively giddy. And I didn't like it one bit.

Though over the years I had often pined for an end to

the constant misery Shamus dragged around with us, "Happy Shamus" was troubling me more than I ever could have imagined. As it turned out, I preferred Hot-Tempered, Hair-Trigger, Rage-Fueled Mood-Swing Shamus. At least that Shamus had patterns to his behavior that I knew quite well. Patterns I was very good at predicting, the most common of which was depression, angst, drink, rage, sleep, depression, angst, drink, rage, sleep, depression … and so on.

But happy? Upbeat? Engaged? *Chipper*? I'd never seen it. Not until that day. So there was no predicting what might come next in the sequence, and that deeply unnerved me. Almost as much as my confirmation of what I'd first suspected—that Sulphur was nothing but a ghost town. Just a few collapsed structures dotted the arid landscape.

The only intact artifact in this harsh wilderness was the dilapidated entrance to an old mine—a large wooden structure built into the side of a mountain in the distance, heavily petrified by the sun but still standing. I stared off at it, squinting against the oppressive glare, and let out a deep exhale. I still remember the particular sting of disappointment I felt—nothing to do out here but watch the tumbleweeds blow by and try not to stroke out.

"Happy birthday to me," I mumbled under my breath with a healthy amount of angst. I would spend my thirteenth birthday in *Sulphur*. After driving for a week straight in a rickety old house on wheels, stopping almost anywhere would have been a welcome change. Anywhere, that is, but the depressing remnants of an abandoned sulfur mine in the middle of a barren wasteland.

That's why when my grandfather asked me to join him on his evening walk—something I almost never did, as he typically never asked—I agreed. At that moment, the only other alternative was watching Shamus cook our dinner on the little portable grill he set up under the RV's yellow and white striped awning, and wonder—and worry—why he was being so helpful. Why everything was off. Why it felt like the axis of the earth had wobbled out of alignment.

Little did I know that on that very day *it actually had ...*

"I said, does it surprise you?" my grandfather asked me as we walked along the dusty road. I was having a hard time concentrating. Life itself had shifted out of focus the moment we arrived. I chalked it up to being in a "desert haze," to the heat and the disappointment. But I still felt badly that I didn't have the foggiest idea what we'd been talking about. A fact he quickly figured out.

"The word *apocalypse* ..." he repeated, more than a hint of agitation in his voice as he wrung his hands—hands that normally rested in a peaceful clasp behind his back. I got the strong impression that for some reason this conversation *had* to happen, and soon.

Cian had been growing increasingly out of sorts as we neared Sulphur. I'd never witnessed him the least bit tense, but that day he was downright stressed, even anxious. For the first time ever and since, he struggled to direct us to our destination, becoming more and more frazzled, almost disoriented, the closer we got. He even argued back when Shamus disagreed with him about our route.

"Just be quiet and drive," Cian chastised him, the sharpest reprimand I'd ever heard come out of my grandfather's mouth. Then I watched in bewilderment as he fought to swallow his pride once it was clear Shamus had been right, somehow knowing the way better than Cian, and that we had to turn around.

It seemed to me Cian was heavily conflicted, as if being in Sulphur was somehow not his choice. But up until the day he asked where I'd like to go and I choose Rugby, we only ever went where *he* decided we'd go. So that too struck me as more than a little strange.

But perhaps most unnerving of all, as we walked along the deserted road that night and he looked skyward at the vast bowl of stars beginning to appear above us in the fading twilight, I got the distinct feeling he was avoiding my eyes— something I couldn't imagine that Cian would *ever* do.

"The word *apocalypse*, Eve—which by definition means 'the lifting of the veil'!" he reiterated yet again, making no attempt to hide his aggravation, and I gave a slow, thoughtful nod. As he gazed up at the sky, I studied the ever-increasing lines on his face. I did this whenever I thought he wasn't looking. For about a year I'd been noticing that his aging was accelerating. But standing there in the barren desert, in the middle of a ghost town, was when it truly started to worry me that I might lose him. I stewed for a moment in the terrible thought: *he's not going to live forever; what happens when he dies?*

"Yes," I admitted as I turned my eyes toward the heavens, trying to put the concerns about that odd day, of everyone's strange behavior, and of Cian's unstoppable aging out of my mind and finally consider what he'd just told me.

"It is surprising," I admitted, and it was—even more so as I let my wheels begin to turn, thinking about how the word *apocalypse* conjured up images of Armageddon, of the destruction of the world. Cataclysmic disaster. Suffering. Death. To learn that it actually meant "the lifting of the veil" was, frankly, more than surprising. I was stunned.

Most every lesson began this way. With Cian upending something I thought I knew. Casually illuminating the many basic things I still had to learn. Drawing me in.

"But, I don't understand," I told him, both of us still staring at the sky.

"And why's that?" he asked. Something he always did, rather than just tell me. I often suspected that Cian had been Socrates in a past life.

I stated the obvious: "Because everyone believes it's about doom and ruin."

"And what does that tell you?" he challenged me.

"That they have it wrong," I said slowly, his gaze finally meeting mine as the fading glow of late evening collapsed into full darkness behind him.

"How might that happen?" he asked.

"If someone … changed it, somehow …" I began to speculate, and almost instantly wondered who might do such a thing, how, and why.

"You're exactly right. It *was* changed, beginning a very long time ago. How it was changed and why are questions for another time. Regardless, to this day, humanity doesn't yet understand this. Like many things, Eve." He spoke tenderly now, and for some reason, he began studying my face very closely, as if he was guiding me through something incredibly important and trying to gauge how much of it I was truly absorbing.

"The literal translation of a word can be quite different from what people come to believe it means over time," he went on. "In truth, it's this way with many words. As for the word *apocalypse*, its origins can be traced back to—"

"Greece. *Apo* meaning '–un,'" I cut him off at the pass the second I knew where he was heading. "And *kaluptein* meaning '-cover,'" I added with confidence, decoding the ancient word from what he'd just told me. "*Apokaluptein*, meaning to uncover," I told him proudly. The range of my intellect was already so vast, and the only thing bigger at that age was my enthusiasm for showing it off.

"Yes, the word *apocalypse* was first used by the Ancient Greeks as *apokaluptein*, 'to uncover'—'lifting of the veil,'" he affirmed. "Which became the source of the Middle English word."

I always listened carefully whenever my grandfather spoke, knowing that his lessons were as layered as onions. He would peel the next one back, and then the next over time, and by this age, I'd already begun to search for what was at the center.

That's when he usually fell silent and watched me. It's what he did whenever he saw a concept taking root, developing inside my mind like the negative of a photograph. Though I had no idea at the time, he already knew I was the oldest soul on Earth and how that made my brain a unique and limitless place. I think he enjoyed putting in certain bits of information and seeing what I would spit out.

"So, an apocalypse is really ... a revelation," I said finally, to which his eyes twinkled. He couldn't help smiling. Not his usual measured grin either. This one was ear to ear.

"That's right," he confirmed, a note of inspiration giving his voice a lift. "A revelation," he repeated slowly, intently, like the word itself was more than just a word. That it was, in fact, the answer. I thought of the Book of Revelation, the last book of the Bible, a prophecy of the Apocalypse. The end. Judgment Day, and the start of a whole new world. I didn't share this thought with him, and the connection I made that day had slowly drifted from my mind over the years.

"Many things have been ... *misinterpreted* through the ages," he said. "Just like words and their meanings, symbols and what they're meant to represent, even our very history, and our legends, myths, and fairytales, these things all get rewritten again and again. Altered. Changed. Reinterpreted. Reinvented to suit a given narrative, to give support to certain ideas and to take it away from others. Words and stories once meant to bring you closer to the truth, to convey knowledge, can instead be used to hide it. These are lies, my dear, plain and simple. I want you to understand that."

He looked at me as he spoke, through my eyes and right into my soul. "Remember, humanity is never crazy about the truth, but deep down it's what they want. Plant this idea in your heart for me, Eve," he said, pressing his hand to the center of my chest, then choosing his next words with great care.

"Humanity *does* want the truth. Let this idea grow in you, slow and steady—like the tree. The knowledge that's forbidden is the all-important truth. You will break the code, Eve. You'll see it before anyone else … and you will expose the greatest lie ever told. That's why you have come."

As Cian turned his face back to the stars, I hardly had time to wonder if I'd just been told my destiny before he issued what sounded a lot like a warning, one seeming to come direct from the cosmos:

"That's why, unlike everyone else, it's not the apocalypse that scares us …" He raised his thick eyebrows and clasped his hands behind his back and walked away, leaving me with nothing but his cryptic words and my own wonder.

'Then what is it that scares us?' I wanted to call after him, but of course I didn't. Those kinds of questions were never answered. They were met with a very special kind of silence, one that somehow instantly dropped the question back in your own lap.

'There is a time for asking and a time for wondering," is all he would have said, likely without even turning around.

So, is it a coincidence then? Irony perhaps? That just a few years later here I am: the Queen of the Apocalypse.

All right, maybe the poster child …

But with everything that happened after Cian left me on my own in Rugby—the tsunami, the blood moons, the unthinkable, and Animus, with my inextricable link to all of it—I've been wondering about that mysterious day in the desert. Wondering about the questions I didn't ask about the Book of Revelation and the Tree of Knowledge, about "the all-important truth" that Cian spoke of and how on Earth I was going to uncover it.

How do you crack a code that you can't even see?

But more than anything else, I wonder about his haunting words. *It's not the apocalypse that scares us.*

Because Cian was certainly right about one thing. I haven't been sacred; I've been terrified.

I'm terrified now, I admit to myself, as I study the two doors in front of me, standing with them a foot from my face. Tall doors, perhaps fifteen feet, hand carved of heavy lumber and fitted with ancient iron fixtures. Side-by-side they form an imposing grand archway—one designed to intimidate no matter which side you're standing on.

Here in Antiquus, in the ancient enclave of old souls, I imagine that everything is thought through—even the doors of my bedroom. After all, it is the bedroom of the girl with the highest Incarnation Number in the world, the girl with the oldest soul on Earth. They should be important doors. They should be very hard doors to pass through, and not because of their size. Because beyond them the rest of this life is waiting for me, and I know almost nothing about what it will look like, though I have a nasty nagging feeling it will be short and painful and filled with strife.

TWO

— ❖ —

Barely breathing, I stare at the wood grain until it begins to melt into the wavy brown lines, until what I see before me is no longer the smooth surface of an elegant door, but the tree it came from—more specifically, the tree's patterns of genetic information, the coded sequences in its rings. As I dissolve into them, marveling at how the swirling lines are encoded with genetic instructions and layers of time, it reminds me of my own DNA, which reminds me of Animus. And as I go deeper into the centuries and eons revealed in the circular patterns of lines, I begin to wonder, what has Animus done? Has it reshaped the world? Where will I fit into it? What is it really calculating? What is it measuring?

My focus abruptly slips into a fuzz of white noise, a feedback loop of static, a mental code blue—another one—

the third one in a row. This will happen at least four or five times.

All I'm trying to do is leave my room. But before I'm able to hold focus long enough, to grab the iron knob, to push the heavy door open, to actually walk myself out into the hallway, my mind will spin into a kaleidoscope of nonsense. Of time and space and DNA. Of shapes and patterns and questions I can't answer. Then it will collapse like this, again and again, reminding me just how badly I've been shattered. How the loss of my grandfather and the thousands of lifetimes rising over my head and submerging me all at once have incinerated my spirit and obliterated my mind.

I hit the only reset button I've got. I think of what I know—my three things, the three most important things in my world. The three things I must build from, my starting points.

The first is a basic one. But mentally, as you might have guessed, I'm in a pretty basic place.

I know that I'm alive.

Reminding myself of this fact, as ridiculous as it may seem, is where I begin again each time. Reminding myself that I wasn't killed by Shamus in Eremis, the overworld where he caused the tsunami and the blood moons and the unthinkable to occur and be reflected here on Earth—

plunging the world into chaos, into believing the apocalypse had begun. Eremis is like a sheet of carbon paper. Whatever is done there is reflected here. It's where Shamus took my grandfather's life in an unforgivable act of cold-blooded evil.

But, I remind myself, *he did not take mine*, even though he had promised to had I proven not to be the waker, as I was proven not to be.

Exactly why he chose to spare my life is one of the many things I do not yet understand. At first I was convinced it was a miracle when Roman, Phoenix, and I ended up back in Antiquus. I was shocked that any of us made it out of Eremis alive that night, but all of us did—save for Cian, of course.

And so I wonder, in between my brain's short circuits and hard resets, why Shamus hadn't killed me when he had the chance. When he stood behind me, sword in hand, as I knelt beside the body of our grandfather, grief struck, paralyzed by the sight of him lying dead. Why hadn't Shamus relieved me of my head the second it became clear that I was unable to wake Cian, and anyone else for that matter, therefore rendering myself useless to my brother?

I'm not sure.

It stands to reason that perhaps I am *not* useless to him. That perhaps Shamus needs me for something. Something he's aware of that I am not.

As frightening as that sounds, I will uncover it, whatever it is. That's the second important thing I know.

I know what I want.

It's a drive so compulsive that it makes everything else I've ever wanted—to go to school, to live in one place, to be normal—seem as ridiculous as the daydreams of a child. I had those desires, yes, but they're gone now. They dissolved, as dreams will do. This is different. This is a singular focus hardwired into my soul, threaded through my DNA, and beating in my heart—to discover the all-important truth, to crack the code, as Cian said I would, exposing the greatest lie ever told.

Yes, that's a tall order for anyone. But it's an even more ludicrous goal for someone having such a rough time opening a stinking door. Given my present state, emotionally crippled and mentally incapacitated, admitting that I plan to accomplish such a herculean task, even just to myself, is remarkably embarrassing.

First, I need to fight my way back. I have to rejoin the world, whatever it looks like now. I have got to find out what's going on and where I fit in to all of it. Which brings me to the third important thing I know.

Order is the first law of the universe.

I'm not sure why I know this exactly. Not sure why it

echoes in my dreams.

Order is the first law of the universe.

Order is the first law of the universe.

Order is the first law of the universe.

Noticing things a bit more, as I have lately, I've begun to suspect that Antiquus is all about *order*, that these words constitute some kind of motto, and that here there's a very distinct order, one that would of course revolve around some common purpose—one everyone is aware of, and a part of. Everyone, that is, except me.

I've been busy losing my mind and finding it again. That's a sort of all-consuming thing, one I don't recommend if it can be avoided. It's taken me to places no one should ever go, transforming me into everything from a demon to a ragdoll.

It's for that reason, I gather, that I've been mostly left alone.

After I watched Ansel and three other men carry my grandfather's small corpse down a tunnel far below Antiquus and lay him on a cold white slab in a bright sterile room, I kind of checked out. I became so disoriented, in fact, that my mind even turned all the people surrounding Cian, Ansel, and the others into strange reptile aliens. Their elongated bright green irises. My blinking, like split-second X-rays, revealed bizarre humanoid skeletons and scales under their skin. That was the last thing I remembered. After that moment, as far as I knew, the world was just hovering in the still silent air around my lifeless body while I quietly slipped into oblivion.

To my surprise, it turns out that life definitely went on.

A person can lose days that way, when they float off into the dark netherworld of grief. As for me, being the hopeless oddball I am, I managed to climb out of that bottomless abyss of mourning only to arrive to a place far worse. A place that lies beyond, home to the most unimaginable depths of human suffering, where every one of my past lives was waiting for me to be relived in graphic detail, a place where I will have to revisit things left unfinished. When I'm ready. When I don't feel like it could suck me right back in. Abasus. It was in Abasus where I lost most of the nearly six weeks of time that's elapsed since Cian's death, in the dark underworld of Earth that's second from the bottom. Last stop before Nirhaya.

When I recently realized that I'd returned, that my worn out and ravaged soul had finally rejoined my equally battered body, the first thing I noticed was my room—my new bedroom here in Antiquus. I saw it in tiny bursts, a millisecond here, a millisecond there, as my eyes began to open again, between the long stretches of darkness.

As my awareness steadily increased, I noticed next that

the pull of sleep had grown as strong as the very force of life within me—I noticed I had a choice. It was a conscious choice, whether to keep living or just stop breathing. When simply waking up became my full time job. Luckily, around the same time, this tiny imperceptible voice coming from somewhere, deep inside perhaps, would gently whisper for me to keep living. It only spoke every now and again, and never with any enthusiasm that I could hear, nor did it offer ideas as to how; that was my cheering section.

And at some point I graduated to placing one foot in front of the other.

That's how I got to where I am now, out of bed, dressed, and about to venture outside, one foot in front of the other. I assume that discovering the hidden code of the universe and exposing the greatest lie ever told will come later. The most critical thing I can do at this moment is not to climb back into bed.

Just minutes ago, I awoke the way I always do now—in a fit of terror to a sharp gasp of air hitting the back of my throat.

My eyes had snapped open to utter darkness. I shifted them rapidly back and forth, one side to the next, again and again, seeing nothing, but feeling something heavy, like a blanket that didn't stop at my skin.

Awake less than a second, I remembered what it was. This feeling.

It was emptiness.

It was the death of my grandfather and the obliteration of my mind. The loss of everything I'd ever known or wanted. And it laid on me like rigor mortis. So heavy and so paralyzing that I barely noticed the reappearance of sleep, when, like a sly fox, it attempted to carry me back off.

There were no windows in my room; it was underground. But imagining there were and picturing vast open windows in every direction, twenty feet tall and letting in crystal blue skies, I flew toward one. It was beautifully arched at the top. The closer I got, the larger I realized it was—the size of an entire city building by the time I was about to float through it. An unseen force behind me began pulling me down. Looking back toward where I'd come from, I saw myself sleeping, aglow in a single shaft of white shimmering light. A moon-colored, silver-gray blaze illuminated me, the clothes clean-lined and earth-toned on my body. I was curled in a ball like a small scared child, surrounded by terrifying pits of darkness on all sides.

Get up. Let's go. This force seemed to urge me from somewhere in the room. But instead, I looked toward the blue skies, planning to keep going into a dream where I couldn't feel this crushing weight of emptiness.

Come on.

This time I heard where it was coming from—the dark corner near the door—and with a sudden jerk, I slammed back into my body and awoke in a single violent jolt.

Uncurling my legs from practically under my chin, I lay flat on my back. I lifted one heavy arm from my side and then the other, and stretched open my hands, seemingly against their will. As I forced my fingers to splay wide apart, I began to feel something—soreness—extending from my cracking wrists to my callused palms and through each finger.

I wondered why my hands were so unbearably sore, and for a few minutes I lay there weighing the effort and energy it would take to investigate and just how badly I wanted to know.

Sitting up finally, light headed and weak, I wondered how long I'd been sleeping. How many times I'd gone in and out. I wondered what I had been dreaming about, why I always woke this way, choking and gasping for air, stricken with terror.

With the thumb of my left hand, I traced a letter M on the palm of my right. I did this every time I awoke, without any idea as to why. Every day, I attempted to reassemble the pieces of the same puzzle as my mind tried to heal, to figure out how to live with all the memories of so many lifetimes constantly buzzing in and out. To retell myself over and over the three important things I knew and begin the daily process of slowly peeling the heaviness away from my bones.

With a resigned sign I focused across the cavernous space, which grew lighter bit by bit as my eyes adjusted, and saw what had been calling me out of sleep. In a dark corner, an object I immediately recognized by its unmistakable shape. *That's right*, I thought. *It's my ax.*

And it's right where I left it ...

So with one last glance at the bed, ax in hand, I push through the double doors. The distinct sweet smell of sandalwood hits me as I open them—such a strong and familiar smell, like the smell of life itself somehow—and as I walk out into the empty hall, it occurs to me that I don't know whether it's the middle of the night or the middle of the afternoon.

My room is on what I believe to be the deepest subterranean level of Antiquus. The reason, I'm guessing, is because of what my Animus test revealed, that my Incarnation Number is 6666. Of course they would put the devil closest to hell.

The long empty corridor starts out flat and gradually

increases in incline. After a few minutes of walking, my heart begins to pound in my chest and my breath becomes heavy, both from the exercise and how much this passageway unnerves me.

The narrow space is dimly lit with an orange glow. Gaslight flames flicker in large glass sconces, affixed at considerable distances to the limestone walls, casting terrible shadows in the dark spaces between them. Wild shadows that seem alive as they dance all along the white stone. Shadows that reveal your state of mind depending on whether you think they look like they want to play with you or kill you. I see nefarious demons swooping about plotting my death. So I cast my eyes downward and keep walking. Staring at the boots on my feet, unlaced snow boots with thick rubber soles, and at the marble floors, which are white with a dull shine, aged and pitted in places, with veins of gray interspersed in subtle patterns. Aside from my rhythmic labored breathing, I only hear one other thing—the scrape of iron being dragged over marble. It's a distinctive metallic whine that tells you what marble is truly made of despite how strong it looks. That just beneath the luster it's chalky and unsound. This noise frays my nerves, but I press on anyway, the incline growing ever steeper.

When the simplest tasks in life feel like trudging through

mud, always at the top of the list are getting out of bed and walking. I've already done both today. Which eases the blow that speaking isn't even in the realm of possibility.

THREE

I haven't spoken in thirty-nine days, not counting today. Today makes forty.

But as I push open another heavy wooden door, this time at the end of the corridor that opens to a vast and sprawling space, the pale yellow hue tells me that it's barely dawn. I imagine the distant winter sun just beginning to break above the Adirondacks, and it hardly seems fair to count today. Not yet anyway. Though I likely won't be talking today either. I'm not sure I remember how or why on earth I'd want to.

It's not that I was keeping track. I wasn't counting off days with little tick marks in neat rows on my wall. Not when I lost my mind the way I did. When I went to *that* place, the one outside yourself, where your soul is exposed and can be ripped to shreds. The place where demons exist.

Where there's no air and the suffering seeps into your lungs like water into a sinking vessel, plunging you to your impending grave on the ocean floor. It's other people, the worried people—and the morbidly curious, of course—who monitor your speaking and eating habits, or lack thereof. They log these things like it's their job, trying to quell the fearful suspicion that it's all they can really do for you, which gnaws at them constantly.

As for me, the person whose mind was lost, flung out of bounds, far beyond any of the known and acceptable places, I hadn't even noticed I wasn't speaking—apparently *that* happens. The only reason I know now is because I heard them say it. Though plenty of people had probably been saying all manner of things since the darkness closed in around me (that's never pretty), I certainly wasn't aware of any of it. And yet for some reason, this one thing managed to break through yesterday morning. It reached me as I marched robotically in the direction of the abandoned hollow that I know to be a few hundred yards to the east. I was dragging this very large ax behind me—just as I'm doing now.

"There goes the lunatic girl. Did you hear? She hasn't spoken in thirty-nine days?" with its faux-hushed tone, as fascinated as it was critical. I became suddenly aware of the stark silence that surrounded me, the vigilant worrisome silence. How I'd been unknowingly keeping it. And it's hard to say which surprised me more—hearing that I hadn't so much as uttered a single word in more than five weeks or realizing that I'd done it without even noticing.

It was another clue that life had marched on, just not for me. Mine took a detour into hell when I witnessed a power-hungry monster, otherwise known as my own brother, sink one razor-sharp end of a sword into the throat of our grandfather, when Cian O'Cleirigh exhaled his last breath and with it released all the memories of all my past lives. He'd somehow been holding them back, shielding me like a mighty dam, his life force protecting mine … until he no longer could.

So if I haven't spoken since that fateful night thirty-nine days ago it's because I have lost my entire family, relived more than six thousand lives, re-died more than six thousand deaths, traveled through dizzying dimensions and multiple realms as well as a few stages too—four different stages to be exact—to arrive at where I am now. I was deep in what I refer to as the stage three "catatonic stage" yesterday morning, when the words broke through and seemingly pushed me into yet another new stage. Each time it happens like this, moving from one stage to the next, it's like staring out at a mysterious mountain view then suddenly being pushed off the edge of a cliff.

Currently I'm in what I'm calling the "bubble stage." Some sounds of life have become present again, though distant and muffled. I can see and hear what's occurring around me, but everything's distorted, words and conversations mere echoes as they bounce off the rubbery outer surface that houses me—like living behind a thick layer of cloudy insulation, stuck in the fuzzy place between sleep and consciousness. I'm generally aware of people's presence, even their activities at times, and out of nowhere, my focus will occasionally sharpen. But mostly it's all just a misty meaningless blur as I float by—a ghost in a balloon at the edge of the universe.

Only one thing is tethering me to the planet—this ax. I look down at my frail, lifeless hand as it grasps the rough wooden handle, and its massive head bumps over rocky patches of ice and snow. This iron beast feels strangely tangled with my past, with my entire existence. Though I don't yet know how.

There came a point when my memory went into lockdown, an overloaded circuit board that reverted to sleep mode to prevent its own obliteration, probably saving me from death by insanity. The problem is, now I can hardly access any files at all, and certainly not at will. Memories just float in and out as they wish.

In this bubble stage, the memories of one lifetime are

like a faint melody compared with the symphonic screams of others. And there are certain lifetimes that come roaring toward the light whenever I so much as lift the lid of my mind—and one lifetime in particular is always barreling toward me faster than the rest: when I watched the man I loved forced to kill himself.

This terrible vision is enough to prevent me from thinking at all. Each time I try, I'm instantly consumed with every shred of the stinging rage and helpless agony I felt as I witnessed his soul, *Roman's soul*, cruelly and slowly bled out of his body, followed by the intolerable, grisly deaths of our children torn apart by wild dogs, all at the hand of Shamus when he walked the earth as Emperor Nero, a very new soul at the time, who burned down his own city just because he wanted to build a bigger palace. I remember watching his face, seeing his own people perish and centuries melt into ash with nothing more than a look of vacant fascination—no idea what gave life meaning, no concept at all, and not remotely curious.

I shake my head and the memory stops.

Chop wood, Eve. Nothing else matters.

Chopping wood feels better than trying to go back in time—and a lot better than the intermittent overwhelming desire to stop breathing.

So I make my way toward the forest that waits for me.

Out past the imaginary boundary, the one I'm not sure that people cross, the one I think I hear a faint gasping at as I cross right now, where a large clearing begins. This is the imaginary boundary that divides Antiquus from, well, *not Antiquus*. From no man's land, I suppose.

What was once New York, I'm beginning to gather, is no longer. What was once New York is perhaps now officially "nowhere," it seems.

But I don't care. Being nowhere is just fine by me. So I march against the flow of an unending migration, a sea of bodies that part very easily around me. My obvious intention, to walk away from Antiquus across the clearing and disappear into the forest, makes the people I pass feel uncomfortable. I can feel it. I can sense their unease, an emanating pulse of apprehension as they scurry toward the welcoming open arms of Antiquus, toward somewhere, toward some kind of future, as I stalk silently into the wilderness with my ax.

It is *my* ax; I'm certain of that. Though I may not know which lifetime I left it in, it was waiting for me in a remote part of the vastness that is Antiquus. I went to find it at some point. I remember how my bare feet looked crunching deep down into the snow, how they were swollen, blistered, and purplish, nearly frostbitten by the time I came to a stop in front of a thicket of ice-covered branches. When I moved them aside, revealing a weathered barn-red shed I somehow knew would be there, the warped doors swung open, and I caught a glimpse of it, a silver glimmer of the long sharp edge, before being consumed with searing pain, the rush of warm water on my feet.

When I awoke the next day, the ax was leaning against the wall near my bed. Right next to the snow boots I now wear on my feet.

I realize then that there's someone here who seems to be watching over me, who shoves me into showers and forces feeding tubes down my throat, who's saved me from myself on multiple occasions as I've resisted like a wild animal—someone whose job it is, I gather, to keep me alive.

Though now I think I'm approaching a place where, more than a stream of nutrients, what I could really use is just a simple hug.

Though I'm not *ready* to be hugged. In truth, I feel like a lit stick of dynamite. But that doesn't mean I don't need one. And needing a hug and not being remotely ready to *be* hugged … those are the people who need hugged the most. Trust me, it's a very rough spot to be in—it's one of the absolute worst.

That is why people chop wood.

It's why *I'm* chopping wood anyway. It must be. It must be somehow safer to let things come up, feelings and emotions, hate, pain, and loss, as I'm forcefully slicing apart solid spruce, hemlock, beech, or pine with a hefty blade of iron. It's probably best that my unbound rage toward Shamus rise to the surface of my being while all other mortal humans are at a safe distance away from me as I chop wood in the sanctuary of this hollow.

The way the trees bend inward, blocking the wind, stills the air around me. My eyes focus on the countless tiny flecks of snow slowly drifting down from the branches above as I become dizzy, overwhelmed, drugged with the feeling I've done all this before—many times before, in other lifetimes. Dragging this very ax to the craggy divot it now rests in, squaring my body to the large ancient stump before me, swinging the twenty-pound iron beast behind me as a thick cloud of frost from my sudden and warm exhale hangs in the air in front of my face, watching the ax sail downward, cutting open the still air like a razor slicing a hole in space, and the thick log splitting lengthwise, a million tiny splinters of wood bursting away on impact.

Breathless, I stop.

I look at the hundreds of fresh logs at my feet and wonder how long I've been chopping. Then it hits me, like a data dump into my brain: it's not the first time this ax is saving my life. Nor will it be the last.

Just then, I see something coming toward me. A figure,

perhaps, but it's too fuzzy to tell, plus the burning in my chest is starting to grab me. This burning is the reason I'm here. This searing unbearable blaze, like the terrible soreness in my hands, tells me I'm alive. The siren song of the ax is grounding me, forcing me down into my body, illuminating this place, this life. Right now. Present time. Burning chest. The only way to stop it would be to stop breathing so hard, but the rapid pounding of my heart demands oxygen, both from the incredible task of chopping and the strange figure that's closing in on me. Through the haze of consuming depression, through the dense fog of overwhelm, through my soul knowing too much and my mind needing to seal shut the vault of time, I stand motionless, arms at my sides, staring out.

I notice a sudden wave of calm come over me. What I'm unaware of is that the ax has dropped out of my hand. Maybe that's what breaks the bubble, the thud of its handle hitting the snowy earth. But something tears the bubble away in an instant implosion, thrusting me completely back into the world in a single pop—everything crisply visible now.

I stand over heaps of busted-up bark like a billion shards of brown sea glass, the remnants of countless thousands of chopped logs, scattered in all directions around the heavy rubber snow boots on my feet. I glance at my hands, chapped, raw, and blistered, more evidence of days or weeks spent chopping. Through clouds of frost from my breath in the pristine air, I look around and see four perfectly symmetrical stacks of cordwood, organized by species of timber, each a good six feet high, maybe more, encircled around me and dusted with the lightest layer of freshly fallen snow.

Just like the logs that fill Roman's arms as he stands motionless before me, so close that the plume of frozen air escaping his mouth converges with mine.

FOUR

— ✦ —

Against a backdrop of glistening white winter, he scans my face with emerald eyes shining like gems. His brow is furrowed, and his chest rises and falls rapidly as he stands before me, struggling to catch his breath. His body seems stiff with shock, his arms filled with logs—the logs I've been chopping. The ones he's obviously been stacking for days, maybe even weeks. Has he always been right here with me? Has he been here all along?

The way he studies me without saying a word, it's like he's wondering whether I can see him or not. As his gaze intensifies, I think that he somehow knows that suddenly I can. From wherever it was I've gone, though my body was always here, my soul has just returned with a silent sonic boom only he heard.

There should be so much to say.

Almost six weeks have passed. I've literally been to hell and back. I haven't the slightest clue what Roman has been through or what has become of the world, and yet I can't find a single word. Maybe it's the shock of seeing him. Maybe after such a long silence I've forgotten how to talk. Or maybe I just realize how unimportant it is to speak. How much you can experience without any words at all. And how little of what we say in this world truly matters.

Whatever it is, in this moment words feel like nothing more than props, too unreal, too fake somehow. It's everything else I notice, the mysterious force pulsating in the space between us, the look in his eyes of sheer awe and wonderment, and the pounding of my heart against my chest. That's what feels real. That's where the truth in this world is revealed, in the things that are hardest to see and the easiest to lie about.

Feeling something shift between us, I watch the look of fascination on his smooth olive face give way to yearning that quickly eclipses everything else in his eyes. I can tell he wants to reach out, to gently brush back my hair, put his arms around my shoulders, to pull me into him and never let go. He doesn't have to say a word. There's an invisible force pulling me toward him, inviting and powerful, drawing me in.

But for some reason, five strange words come out of my

mouth instead. Clear and calm, they decide to escape all on their own.

"I wasn't unfaithful to you," I say, to his obvious surprise, and to my own, sounding unlike myself, almost mechanical.

After a beat of disbelief, his low voice, tender and more familiar to me now than ever before, seems to rise from the center of his heart.

"It's okay," he reassures me, like no explanation could be necessary for any possible thing in the whole world. A river of compassion spills from his clear green eyes.

But he's wrong. Dead wrong. Deep inside I know this matters.

"No. Roman I want you to understand something," I manage. My voice is having trouble keeping up with my brain, and my brain is having trouble keeping up with my heart. "I did not cheat on you," I insist, trying to reframe what is a very particular sentiment—something coming straight from my soul directly to his but traveling through a signal that's intermittently scrambled.

Searching my face, he finds only frustration. Unsure of what I'm getting at, he shakes his head and lets out a little sigh. His inability to understand produces this tiny burst of warm air that escapes from his dark pink lips in a cloud of frost. So sweet, so familiar, it makes my pulse quicken and something deep inside the center of my belly start to stir from a kind of primordial sleep.

"Listen, whatever it was that you had with Jude," he starts again, "or ... whatever you *have* with him ..." he concedes, then breaks off in spite of himself.

If the heart has a version of what people call "the mind's eye," then it's through that filter that I now see Roman, with an eerie intuitiveness, and this isn't how he imagined our first encounter in six weeks going. This isn't what he'd like to be talking about. It kills him. It does, just the thought of Jude and me. The idea that I may love Jude ... that I even could. Roman's never lived a lifetime without loving me, never witnessed me share my love with anyone else.

"Jude is your fate; I know that," he recites like lines from a script, words he says because they're on the page, not because he wants to be saying them.

"I'm not talking about Jude," I tell him, a few words from my own script, things written on secret pages—ones I've never shown him before.

I take the logs he's still holding in his arms and set them on the snowy ground beside us. When I straighten back up, his gaze has intensified along with his desire to understand. I look deep into his face as I move a half-step closer. Then I reach out and grab both of his hands. We're only inches apart now, and the touch of his skin, holding a part of him, grounds me even further, anchoring me deeper into this world, giving me clarity and making what I must say easier to find.

I take a deep breath. "I'm talking about … Ada," I say slowly, and then let the word sink in.

When I see his thoughts begin to shift off Jude and I and onto the lifetime we shared as William and Ada Lovelace, I go on, "I never cheated on William … *on you*," I say, watching how it brings him into that life, the highs and the lows, the hurt and dysfunction returning along with his heartbreak and the painful memories—everything we shared together then.

His eyes turn from mine, staring past me.

"Why are you telling me this now?" he asks, and I begin to wonder myself. Why is this the first thing I feel compelled to say to the one person in this world who's never left my side, in this lifetime or any other?

Uncertain, I press on. "I was your wife," I begin to explain to Roman, to William, and he returns his emerald eyes to mine, leery but listening. "And though that life was a difficult one for me, and Ada wasn't an easy person to love, I was still your wife. That vow meant everything to me."

I watch a softening come over him, a blanket of relief

beginning to fall over his entire body.

"You *never* did?" he asks, still skeptical, understandably, needing to hear it once more to accept what I'm telling him. I feel like I'm holding his beating heart in my hand, and that I can do whatever I please with it. I feel myself taking possession of this incredible power—just as Ada did. A power that rises up through the earth from another dimension and imbues a woman with a godlike force over a man's mind, heart, and body. I once used it to scar the very same heart I can now use it to mend.

Apparently, it is my soul's first order of business.

"I wasn't good to you. I played mind games, *very knowingly*. You were no match for me. I was *very* smart you know," I quip, attempting to lighten the intensity swirling around us.

"I know," he chides, sarcastic, his bitterness raw. "What else?" he demands, wanting to know more. Needing to know everything.

"I toyed with your affection, willfully. With very little remorse," I admit. His eyes are wounded and doubtful. "None," I confess, and he nods his head. I can see it all making sense to him. "You weren't a narcissist or a workaholic; I just convinced you that you were. I called you those things because that's what I was, what Ada was ... and those were the things I despised most about myself. I was a person in a lot of pain, so I escaped into my work, but the pain always returned, demanding to be felt. And what I did was a very unloving thing. I shoved it off on you. I took my pain, my hurt, my wounds, my sense of inadequacy, the father who left when I was a baby and the mother who couldn't be bothered to raise me, the unhappiness within myself that was like an endless abyss, and I made them all into yours."

I watch his eyes burn red and then well with the tears of another lifetime, ageless tears, tears of relief from his soul finally allowing those old, deep cuts to heal.

I hug him. I hug William without a thought or a moment of hesitation. I just pull him toward me. No longer the lit stick of dynamite I once was, right now I feel like Mother Earth herself. Like a force of nature able to manifest miracles of healing, to restore in a new season what I ravaged in the last. My cheek on his chest, my arms wrapped around his back at his waist. He pulls me in closer, fitting my head perfectly in the curve of his throat.

"Is there anything else?" He asks after several minutes of quiet.

"Just that you tried," I say, still locked in his embrace. "You never stopped trying, but I wouldn't let you love me. I couldn't allow myself to be loved. And I couldn't love, not really, not even you ... It's a prison on earth, Roman, not knowing love. But I *was* devoted. Always. I wanted to give you at least that much. It was the best Ada could do." I part enough to look up at him.

"I believe that," he nods, staring down into my eyes.

"Anyway, you said you were never sure Ada was actually unfaithful … and she never was. She just wanted you to think that she had been," I tell him, disclosing the last of it and feeling the final release for both our souls as all the burdens of that lifetime dissolve into something else. Into knowledge and understanding, an instant deepening of our transcendent and paranormal connection.

"Do you remember everything? All your lifetimes, all the ones we shared?" he asks me, our bodies so close, eyes locked. He's making no attempt to hide what he's curious about—whether I remember everything that he does about the nearly three hundred lifetimes we'd spent together.

"Yes and no. It comes and goes in waves. The memories seem to just appear, certain memories at certain times. Then they recede. They drift back out, far away from me to where I can't really see them at all."

"Is it overwhelming?" he asks with incredible tenderness, reaching out to caress my cheek and sending a stream of butterflies soaring from one side of my stomach to the other.

"It's manageable."

"It's manageable now..." he suggests, venturing to clarify what I'm afraid he's observed—the physical fallout of my recent and unplanned trip to hell.

"Right. When Cian died, they crushed me all at once," I admit, but it's all I'm ready to say about that. I suddenly get a rush of pins and needles all over my face and arms. As I feel myself go pale and dizziness swell from my chest to my head, he tightens his grip on my elbows to steady me.

"Eve, you need to eat something." He's absolutely right. I notice all at once. I'm starving. Hunger like I haven't felt since the moment I first met him burns through me, the pain second only to the overwhelming surge of frost I feel, the staggering sting of bone-chilling cold.

Tuned into my needs in an almost telepathic way, his arms are around me, he's guiding me back out of the subzero air before I even say a word. Under the protection of his body's warmth, we head out from under the canopy of trees, back toward Antiquus—toward the rest of this lifetime, whatever it holds, leaving the ax behind us laying half buried in the snow.

"It's going to take you some time to adjust," Roman concedes. When like a glimpse into a mythical world, the staggering structure on the other side of the clearing fills my view. Roman steadies me as I stumble backward at the sight of the impenetrable citadel, how it appears to extend to the ends of the earth. How it rises up out of the ground as if it's trying to greet the gods who surely created it, how it sprawls out over the unending hills behind it like a colossal dragon lying on its belly, pretending to sleep. The white marble towers and soaring walls of vivid limestone are blinding, even from a distance, and I easily see how every corner is shored up with heavy brackets of iron flanked by rows of regal buttresses. But it's the breathtaking spires, which I remember seeing when Phoenix and Roman and I first pulled up on the night Cian would die, that shock me most. They look like luminescent gold daggers, their ascension seeming endless as they pierce the clouds.

When we approach the mountainous entrance gates, forged of solid bronze and gleaming golden in the sunlight like a portal to a celestial kingdom, Roman looks with concern at the expression on my face.

"You're disoriented."

"Beyond," I whisper, unable to take my eyes off the splendor before me, unable to process its vastness, the kingdom of kingdoms that is Antiquus.

"How is this possible?" I marvel more than ask, taking in the high walls of stacked limestone, the unending fortress of turrets and towers with a thousand tiny windows here and there, feeling like I'm seeing it all for the first time.

"You'll get used to the size of this place—and everything else here," Roman promises, his arm securely around my shoulders, hurrying me along. "You'll be fine. Everything's going to be fine. You'll adjust."

"Why do I get the feeling you're trying to convince yourself?" I ask as we walk past a small group of dark-robed men, and I see on Roman's face all the things I don't know yet that he does. The worry that I have a whole new life now, one I know nothing about. One he worries that I may not like.

I start to panic. "Everyone else has had time to adjust."

Roman pulls me closer against his side. We skirt past the massive front doors, breezing by another group of people—men, women, and children this time, twenty or so, dressed in white robes tied with brown belts, their hands resting at their sternums in prayer position.

As I crane my neck to glare at everyone we pass, Roman briskly walks me along. We follow a white pebble path next to a high limestone wall until we come upon a small arched wooden door. A discrete side entrance, almost normal-sized I think, until I see the breathtaking garden immediately to my right. A maze of slate walkways through rows of manicured shrubs. Against the thick blanket of pristine glittering snow that covers the ground, this strangely vivid garden looks straight out of Wonderland.

"White Christmas roses," I remark, a burst of nostalgia pushing my thoughts to someplace else, almost abducting me to Jamestown, Virginia, 1615.

"I know." Reverence in his voice, Roman confirms more than just the variety of flower. It's the memory of our brief marriage and time together at Varina Farm, where he grew the first strains of tobacco for export and stunning white Christmas roses for me, spectacular blooms with their outward-facing pure white petals each delicately kissed with edges of bright lime and brilliant yellow centers.

Roman and I breathe in that lifetime through the familiar sweet fragrance, haunting floral pheromones with the power of time travel. I marvel at how every shrub is absolutely covered with roses—each rose more captivating than the next and more majestic, all displaying themselves proudly beyond thick clusters of waxy blue-green leaves.

My eyes land on a rose just a few feet from us. Out of instinct I reach for it. But Roman raises his hand to grab mine. He gently pulls it back, shaking his head with an almost imperceptible no.

Then, sounding overly formal, robotic even, as he glances around us then opens the wooden side door to usher me inside, "The first thing I should probably tell you Eve, is the year."

FIVE

— ✦ —

Stepping out of the brisk winter air, out of the hypnosis of the garden, and into a darkened room that might be some kind of kitchen, I have more than a few questions.

"What do you mean, the year?"

But when he flips a switch on the wall, five stunning crystal chandeliers hung across the mahogany-coffered ceiling illuminate the gargantuan space with a warm inviting glow. Hundreds of gleaming copper pots catch my eye. Polished to a high shine, they hang in a long neat row over a procession of gas ranges squatting like clawed beasts.

My eyes drift up to beautiful red-brick arches artfully concealing the industrial steel hoods above each range, and a new smell hits my nose—and my hungry stomach—stealing every question from my mind. The scent of warm vanilla cinnamon rolls and spiced apple pie. It almost pulls me across the black and white checkered marble floor, enticing me to walk deeper into the warm comfortable space.

I try to shrug off the overwhelming Alice in Wonderland vibe I started feeling the moment we crossed the threshold of Antiquus's gates. Telling myself to focus, to not be seduced—though so far most everything has been notably seductive—to not lose myself, to keep hold of the steadiness I've worked so hard to regain.

Maintain your focus, your three things, I tell myself.

Turning around to where Roman is still standing near the door we entered, I ask about what he just told me.

"How is it a different year? I only lost six weeks …"

He nods.

"It was decided, based on … a historic astrological discovery, that we'd go to a thirteen-month calendar," he explains, his words seeming curated, but not by him. "It's a more accurate way of keeping time."

His demeanor is gentle, protective, like I may shatter into a million pieces if he tells me too much too quickly.

"Thirteen months … *a lunar calendar* …" I say as he takes my hands in his.

He smiles. "That's right, of course. Is there anything you don't know?" he wonders aloud, studying me, the way I process information, pulling whatever I need from some limitless stash of knowledge.

"Thirteen months, each with twenty-eight days. Twelve months was never accurate," I mumble to myself. "It was the thirteenth sign of the Zodiac … in 2011, right? Ophiuchus, the constellation called the serpent bearer," I say, partly to Roman and partly just talking out loud as I sort through my mind.

OPHIUCHUS

"Exactly," Roman whispers out in amazement, but I don't stop to feel flattered. I keep searching for more meaning, more information. Anything else I remember learning about Ophiuchus—from when Cian mentioned the discovery. It was … *the symbolism*, I recall suddenly, which he seemed so intent on teaching me; the real meaning of Ophiuchus he specifically framed as "surprising," just like the true meaning of *apocalypse*. Though most often associated with evil incarnate, the serpent actually represents great healing and the knowledge of immortality and enlightenment. And according to the ancient Romans, Jupiter, not wanting humanity to know of their own immortality, killed the serpent bearer with a lightning bolt.

"What is it," Roman asks, startling me out of the thought just as it turned ominous.

"Huh?"

"Come on, what were you thinking?" He tilts his head, wondering. But I don't see a point in explaining all of this to Roman, not yet anyway—I don't even know whether or how any of it connects.

"It makes sense, but well, the lunar calendar has *always* made more sense than the solar calendar. Why this change? Why right now?" I ask him.

"It wasn't something *everyone* wanted," he concedes with instant regret on his face. Like already he's said too much. And I start to become sure that he's trying to protect me from something.

"What do you mean?" I press, but by his deep inhale and overwhelmed look I can tell he doesn't know where to start. Growing irritated, I skip to my next question: "So how does changing to a lunar calendar suddenly change the year?"

"It doesn't. I mean, this part makes less sense to me. It was decided, in order to leave behind all the tragedy of not just the events of the last few months but the last two thousand years … all the war, and the bloodshed … and based on how much everything has changed and will be different *forever*, going forward—"

"Someone is trying to erase history," I say, an interruption he doesn't deny but also doesn't seem to want to comment on either. "So what year is it?" I ask, my tone much sharper than normal.

"It's … Year Zero. It isn't about erasing history. It's a brand-new beginning. The dawn of a new world," he explains in a tone of measured optimism.

I squint my eyes and cock my head, wondering how, with words that don't sound like his own, he can stand there and tell me that it's not erasing history while describing something that sounds an awful lot like erasing history.

Studying the look on my face, a mixture of irritation and hunger, he brings me over to an upholstered high-back chair alongside a long wooden table in the center of the room. A room that I notice is beginning to spin.

"I'll explain everything," he promises me, removing his still snow-dusted jacket to reveal a long sleeve green button-down that perfectly mimics the color of his eyes. He offers to take my coat too, but I'm still far too cold. And in truth, part of me doesn't feel safe enough. A little whisper inside says I haven't quite decided whether I'll be staying here or making a break for it. I want to trust Roman, of course. I want to trust him with my life and with my heart too. On the one hand, he's more than earned it—I'm likely only alive because of him. And he clearly cares for me, tremendously, to a degree that defies any expectations I could have ever had. But on the other hand, here we are again. He's withholding things, just like he did in Rugby, deciding exactly what I should know and when I should know it. I'm suddenly reminded of how he neglected to tell me my IN when he knew all along. How he even lied straight to my face when he told me he didn't know. Even if it was to protect me, it still affected my trust.

As Roman crosses back into the kitchen, I study him in all his tall handsomeness, shaking my head slightly in disbelief at the sheer perfection of his appearance and the spectacular way it feels to be in his presence, how it's equally exciting and soothing. It's hard to stay mad.

With a sweet half-smile back at me, he opens one of the big stainless steel refrigerators. After taking out butter and eggs, he glides over to a pantry and disappears into it, emerging seconds later like the rebirth of the Greek god Adonis, with a white apron tied around his waist—just like the night we first met—and a loaf of bread swinging gently from each hand.

"But first, dear Eve, we eat," he says to my starving body's relief, his effortless charm shining through his dazzling eyes. I let out an audible sigh at this captivating boy before me, who now somehow looks much more like a man than the last time I saw him, and resign myself to his beguiling smolder, to my sudden and overwhelming lust for every bit of him, and to the galactic power of his soul's imprint on mine.

"Brioche," he whispers, sweet as the sugary bread itself. "It's my secret ingredient for making the best French toast you've ever tasted." He looks around the empty space in a serious way, as if to keep his secret recipe safe, further disarming me. Making me smile, even laugh a little bit in spite of myself, in spite of everything I still don't know— my first real laugh in a very long time.

The stack of warm caramelized toast he piled on a large silver platter, topped with creamy butter, gooey syrup, and a dusting of powdered sugar didn't stand a chance. Roman ate a hearty amount by any standard, five or six pieces, but it was nothing compared to me. Like I'd never eaten before, I filled my plate again and again with what was hands-down the best French toast in the world, somehow simultaneously soft and crispy, sweet and salty.

"How is it so deliciously chewy and yet also dissolves like cotton candy?" I marvel through a full mouth.

After he finishes eating he sits back, arms crossed, watching happily as I enjoy the feast he's made. I can see that taking care of me, in any and every way, fills his heart with something he can never get enough of.

As soon as I finish, finally unable to eat any more, he starts talking.

First he confirms what I'd already suspected. Over the course of the last month and a half—after the second blood moon rose into the sky at midday and the unthinkable simultaneous loss of every unborn life on Earth, and with no subsequent pregnancies occurring—fear officially won. All semblance of civil society on every continent around the world utterly collapsed.

Then after Cian's death, things went from very bad to even worse.

"Beyond how everyday people were slaughtering one another for water and anything else, government remnants and emergent warlords were committing mass genocide in their misguided attempts to bring order—with nothing and no one to stop them from decimating enormous groups of people who weren't falling into line. So when Animus began to arrive, most believed right away it was the answer."

"And they were promised food and shelter … safety …" I lead him, finding the gaps and holes in what he's telling me out of instinct. Searching for power and motives, as Maricielo taught me.

"Yes, of course, but—"

"Roman, you don't really believe, do you? The whole thing about Animus, how it's some divine fix, the last rescue boat for a humanity that's—"

"I don't know. I mean, since Animus began sorting people and ending unordered soul assimilation all over the world, no more unexplained events have happened. There's been absolute peace on this planet. I mean, when is the last time we could say that?"

"Sure," I say, "but there's just one major problem. The events and the unthinkable aren't unexplained phenomena." Seeing his obvious surprise and confusion, I realize that he doesn't know. Oh my god, he doesn't know.

"What?" he asks, shaking his head.

I take a deep breath, not knowing where to begin. "Remember … in the hallway on the first day of school when something seemed to happen to me, but I never told you what? When you knew I was keeping a secret from you?"

"I remember."

"That was the moment Shamus entered into Eremis for the very first time. It caused a shift. I felt it throughout my entire body. It allowed his insults back into my head. Cian would banish them to Eremis, and they always stayed gone, until that moment when what Shamus said to me that morning came flooding back. You saw it on me, the shock and the fear. But I couldn't explain it to you. Not unless I wanted you to run screaming in the other direction and never look back, which I very much didn't. I wanted you to think I was normal. I wanted you to like me," I confess, realizing how free I feel I can be with Roman—how honest I want to be with him, how completely intimate.

"That's never been a problem," he admits quietly, putting his warm hand on top of mine and causing my heart to skip.

"Well I didn't know that then," I say, trying to refocus, "and I also didn't know what it meant at first, the sudden return of his words to my mind, the sick feeling I got. But we figured it out later, Phoenix and I. And Jude," I add for the sake of accuracy, though I hate how the mere mention of Jude's name so clearly unsettles him. "We learned that Shamus caused what we call 'The Events' in Eremis that morning. Using weapons from another plane, Roman, he killed something sacred, something very beautiful," I pause, swallowing a rush of grief that suddenly swells in me over the crimes against humanity committed by my own brother.

"What does that have to do with The Events?" he asks,

struggling to piece it together and showing me something else. Six weeks ago, before living in Antiquus, Roman would have already figured this out.

"The effects of what Shamus did in Eremis rippled into our world," I explain to him slowly, "directly resulting in the tsunami and the blood-red moons."

As I study Roman's eyes to see whether he understands what I'm telling him, I begin growing certain that he's unable to read between the lines. He's too invested in what he's being told here. So, I waste no time spelling it out for him.

"If this place is built on Animus being the remedy for *unexplained* celestial acts of aggression on an inherently flawed human race, then this place is built on a lie."

He stares at me like something is clicking inside him.

"Nothing is unexplained, Roman," I reiterate, watching his eyes and seeing in them that he's coming around.

"It's the same with the unthinkable," I press. "That was Shamus as well. Roman, he caused it all."

He nods, and it seems he does believe me, but I can tell he's still struggling with something. Perhaps it's something else altogether.

"What are you thinking?" I ask, growing worried by his silence and by the way he averts his eyes from mine. "Tell me. Roman, *please*," I beg, taking his hand in mine. Beyond my strong feelings for him, past and present, he's my closest—and perhaps my only—ally. The one person I know is on my side, and I'm growing worried I may have just turned him against me.

"I always knew everything about Shamus," he finally says. "Why didn't I know this?" He seems lost in thought, somewhere far away.

I breathe out the anxiety that was building up. At least I know he believes me about what really happened. That Shamus caused the supposed apocalypse, and that Animus isn't miraculously generating peace. Everything else we can deal with.

"I'm keeping a very long list of all the things I don't know," I tell him with unmasked relief in my voice. "I'll add that to it, okay?"

I smile, trying to coax him back from someplace else. Eventually it works. He shakes off the shock of everything I just told him and the worry of why he didn't already know.

"Tell me more about what's happening now," I ask him.

"Every surviving human and everyone born in the future—when conception begins happening again, that is—will live in Antiquus, if they're an old soul, or in Primitus, if they're a new soul."

Everyone, with just one exception.

"I'm the only new soul living here in Antiquus," he says with a distinct hush to indicate that this is not exactly public information. According to Roman's Animus Test, this is his two hundred ninety-ninth lifetime, which makes him something called a "King Soul," the oldest of the new souls.

He's talking rapidly now, with no more worry that I'll shatter like glass. "My record has been altered. I'm now 'Roman Alexander Davidson, IN 300, Sage Soul, the newest group of old souls.'" He rolls up the sleeve of his shirt, exposing his muscular forearm, the sight of his bare olive skin causing another unexpected pulse of something wild and innate deep in my belly, and reveals a tattoo. From the crook of his elbow to his wrist, the Roman numeral CCC is written in soft green ink, and everything starts falling into place in my mind.

Then Roman confirms what I'd already figured out, that he's the one who's been taking care of me, day and night, for the past six weeks.

"That's the only reason I was allowed to stay," he explains. "It became clear early on that, though you were gone ... someplace else ..." He struggles to describe what I appeared to be experiencing, then abandons the impossible effort. "You weren't going to let anyone else near you, so ... they didn't really have a choice." He smirks. "A bit defiant, but it meant I got to stay here with you."

"Skepticism, defiance, and civil disobedience are noble means when seeking self-determination," I say, feeling the abrupt need to remind myself, and to reinforce to Roman that his defiance was self-determination, a noble thing in and of itself, not just because it meant he got to stay with me. He tilts his head.

"Maricielo," I say, "he taught me that." And seeing how Roman's face immediately turns pale and how he reaches instinctively for my hand, I know—

"He's gone," Roman confirms, worry in his eyes that grief will snatch me again. "I'm sorry; I know how close you were to him."

"Yes, I was," I breathe out, reeling with shock, but what Roman doesn't know is that with both Cian and Maricielo gone, I suddenly feel the dead weight of responsibility even more than grief, like I'm the last bastion of truth in a world I sense is swiftly being made over by lies.

I feel like the serpent bearer. An overwhelming thought.

It's one thing to be holed up in my room trying to rally myself, making imaginary plans to one day uncover some veiled supreme truth, expose an earth-shattering lie, and fulfill a shrouded divine prophecy. It's another entirely to be thrust down that daunting path on the very same day. Especially given how narrowly I made it out of bed this morning.

And all I see in my mind now is a lightning bolt.

I ask about Phoenix and her sisters and Fiorella. Roman tells me that Fiorella and Zeppelin are here, that he's seen them a handful of times but never close enough to talk, and that he doesn't know about Phoenix and Sequoya.

"Go on," I urge him, needing something else to focus on so that I don't just turn and run.

As usual, Roman gives me what I need. "They created a new record of my test."

"Because all IN numbers are public information," I remember from what we were told in Rugby.

"Exactly. I proposed the idea when it became clear I had to stay with you. They're pretty concerned about what happens to you."

"Who is?"

"Everyone, actually." He rubs the back of his neck, looking stressed.

"But who created the false record of your Animus test?"

"One of the leaders here."

"Who? And why is everyone so concerned about what happens to me? Last I remember, I wasn't very popular." I know I don't have to remind Roman, but I do anyway, checking to see that I'm not crazy. "I was being framed as the antichrist, if I recall correctly."

"That was then."

"What's changed?"

"I told you, Eve. *Everything.*"

SIX

He's only just begun telling me about the collectives, the four types of souls here at Antiquus, when we hear a series of loud bells ring out, reverberating off the copper pots and sending a jolt of adrenaline rushing through me.

"What is that?" I ask. "Some kind of signal?" I guess, frantically.

"Conclave," he says, failing to mask the alarm in his voice as he scrambles into the kitchen with our dishes.

"What's Conclave?" I ask, returning the eggs and the butter to the refrigerator.

"It's a gathering of everyone, from every collective."

"Do we have to go?" I ask.

"No, it's not mandatory, but it's—" He breaks off, shaking his head. "This is unscheduled," he finally adds in a grave tone, then ushers me out of the kitchen through a different door than we entered. It leads, I can only assume, deeper into the staggering castle—and, I'm quite certain, deeper down the rabbit hole.

"They're never unscheduled," he informs me with a hushed voice of manufactured calm that's betrayed by the worry I read on his face and how his hand is moist with sweat and so tightly laced with mine. If he's trying not to cause me to panic, it's far too late for that.

"Nothing is ever unscheduled," he adds as we wind through a dark corridor, heading toward a light glowing in the distance. His eyes dart nervously down to my puffy white jacket, and I remove it in one quick swipe. Roman tucks the bulky coat under his arm as discretely as he can.

We exit the corridor into a stone hallway. Dark tapestries—enormous Renaissance murals—line the walls all the way from the vaulted ceiling down to the marble floor. The only source of light is from gas-powered, cast-iron lanterns interspersed every twenty yards or so, dangling overhead from their long chains. Each tiny orange flame glows brilliantly but not nearly bright enough to illuminate so large a space; they leave a shadowy dimness, one I'm grateful for.

A sea of people wash through the hall, and we dissolve into the mass of humanity near the back of the pack. We're walking briskly, at the same pace as everyone around us, but Roman and I don't exactly blend in.

Everyone is dressed in robes like the ones I saw outside, and in some cases capes of black, white, or green. Roman's shirt is the right green color but the wrong garment. And no one is wearing anything close to resembling my earth-tone shirt and pants. Also, their faces are awash with serenity, unlike Roman's wide-eyed, heart-pounding look of controlled panic that surely matches my own. And each person, save for Roman and me, has wireless headphones covering his or her ears and holds a small tablet.

Hiding as best we can at the rear of the advancing crowd, we leave the hallway and enter into a new area—a stunning place that Roman quietly tells me is the Common Area. It's a breathtaking basilica of clearly hallowed antiquity with a colossal rotunda and frescos of cherubs and angels. It's about as "common" as the Sistine Chapel. It figures that in Antiquus, an ancient Gothic cathedral would be considered a common area.

Roman's eyes begin darting around as if he's looking for someone. He moves toward several men, bespectacled gray-haired older fellows in long dark-green robes.

Brushing up against me is another man with salt and pepper hair. Under his green cape is a matching button-down shirt, just like the one Roman's wearing, and something about him is hauntingly familiar. Behind his glasses, his eyes flick up to meet mine and then quickly drop back to the floor. But I see a small smile creep onto his face.

As the sea of bodies flows to the right, we enter some kind of great hall. From behind Roman and with the hordes of other people in front of me, I can't see much of it yet. Though I have no trouble hearing the music playing. It's loud, dramatic, patriotic music with bugles, violins, and horns, and everyone around me removes the headphones from their heads.

To my right is a large sign that reads SIT ANYWHERE YOU LIKE.

As more and more people start to be seated I catch a glimpse of the vast circular structure with three sections of raised seating surrounding a round center stage at ground level, the clear focal point.

It's modeled after the theaters of ancient Rome.

As he keeps me close, his soft warm hand tightly enmeshed with mine, I get the hint that Roman's trying to hide me. So I duck even farther behind him, my face pressed in between the shoulder blades of his tall burly body.

A brilliant green flag hangs above our seats. It's emblazoned with a strange symbol in a pearl white color. There's some writing too, words I can't make out while looking straight up at it. The lights begin to slowly dim from their stark bright glare.

"The symbol of Sage collective," Roman whispers, nodding to the flag above us, then discretely pointing out that everyone in all the rows around us is wearing the same emerald hue as Roman's shirt.

I glance around the massive circular amphitheater, seeing other flags, each of their colors matching the robes of the people seated underneath them.

"Dragons," Roman whispers, pointing with a hand against his chest to the section to our right, where a large black flag bears another strange symbol, this one emblazed in red. Like the Sages, there are men, women, and children of every race, creed and kind, all dressed in the matching black robes of their collective.

Above the eerie symbol on the black flag reads DRAGON SOUL—and above that, POWER, ACHIEVEMENT, EXPANSION, each separated by a vertical line.

Directly across from us hangs a white flag bearing a symbol in luminescent gold. This section is for those people I saw earlier, the ones wearing the flowing white robes with long brown beads hanging from the belts at their waists. Just like the Dragon's flag, the bold lettering above the symbol reads MOUNTAIN SOUL.

The three words on the bottom below the odd boxy shape: ETHEREAL, SURRENDERED, ENLIGHTENED.

"What's *that* flag?" I whisper into Roman's ear, pointing to the flag hanging down over a chair—a throne—sitting empty in the very center of the vast hall.

"The gold-colored one—right there." I think I catch the word "Zodiac" at the top just before the lights dim completely, enveloping the grand space and the tens of thousands of people in total darkness and perfect silence.

"That's *your* flag," Roman whispers, squeezing my hand for comfort, but it doesn't stop the blood from rushing out of my head and trying to leave my body through my feet. If that's my flag, is that my seat—that elaborate throne, alone, out in the center? My heart starts beating faster, and my mind is racing with questions when a soothing voice begins to speak:

"*World ... peace ...*" I recognize the smooth tone immediately. It's Sourial, the woman we saw on the monitors in Rugby, the one who first told us about Animus.

A 3-D hologram of Earth appears out of thin air, the beautiful blue and green planet seemingly close enough to reach out and touch. It rotates at a slow majestic pace.

"*Finally achieved ...*" she continues, as via hologram images, we descend from space down through the atmosphere and explore the world—a transfixing aerial view of rainforests, pristine rivers and oceans, snow-covered rocky-topped mountains, and scientists in laboratories, happy white-coated smart-looking people in a state-of-the-art lab swirling solutions in glass beakers and looking optimistic, after which a few small children run happily and carefree through a meadow.

"After countless millennia of tragedy, suffering, and war …" The meadow dissolves into a montage of scenes from one deadly natural disaster to the next. In rapid-fire succession it's the worst fury Mother Nature has dished out over the last century, catastrophic earthquakes, raging mudslides, F5 tornados, destructive hurricane winds and deadly storm surges, floods, typhoons, cyclones, and uncontrollable wildfires, which then gives way to raw footage of one bloody human conflict after the next. From the guns and planes and grisly deaths of World War I to the bloodbath of D-Day in graphic detail, and from the shock and horror of Pearl Harbor and Vietnam dragging on, to our interminable conflicts in the Middle East. Then two enormous passenger planes fly in, right over our heads, aimed at the World Trade Center towers that have appeared before us, striking them, desperate souls jumping to escape the burning buildings, shown falling all the way to the ground. And when the towers collapse, it's as if they're falling right on our heads, as if we're standing at Ground Zero looking straight up, and I'm struggling to wrap my mind around how this impossible footage even exists, how it was recorded in the first place, how it survived, and why I've never seen it before.

Then the tsunami wave, hundreds of feet tall, begins rising, just as large as the real one must have been, and like a groaning monster, it smashes through a small coastal town, blasting everything and everyone in sight to splinters. And the eerie blood moon rises, filling the vast circular space so close to my face that I lean back, and it lingers there, wobbling disturbingly. But it's the graphic footage of the horrifying Unthinkable, millions of women all around the globe simultaneously doubled over, writhing in agony from the excruciating pains of sudden labor, their babies being forcibly expelled from their bodies, the blood and the horror, and the dead infants like mountains of dolls, their mothers, and the whole world, wailing, screaming for mercy, torn apart by heartbreak and wrecked with fear. The vivid scenes appear so lifelike and are so haunting, reintroducing these traumas in holographic high-definition. A swell of primal fear deep in my gut, almost animalistic, like I'm clawing at a ledge as I dangle over certain death, gives a concrete weight to all the chaos of the world, the danger, and the unpredictability. I try to slow my breathing and suppress my trembling. Roman places his other hand on top of the hand he's already holding, but nothing helps.

"*No more confusion, no more pain ...*" Sourial's soothing

words fade in as the disturbing images slowly ebb into darkness. I find myself wanting for her voice. Feeling almost lost until I hear it.

"*We will never forget.*" Her words are sober, solemn, and I'm clinging to them.

"*Out of chaos comes order.*" Her voice is a cool breeze. It's as light as air.

Then, appearing out of the darkness like the northern lights dancing on a canvas of deep purple sky, an ethereal Animus symbol glows blue, surrounded by absolute void, spinning majestically, just like the earth had. The more I stare at it, the calmer I feel. Before long, my breathing has slowed, and my hand loosens its grip on Roman's.

"*Order is the first law of the universe.*" The holographic sentence flies out like a comet, blazing around the symbol, orbiting then plunging through it, and then settling into place arched above. The idea of order is tranquilizing, like a powerful drug to the brain.

"*Pheumachronology for world peace,*" she announces victoriously, and that phrase shoots into view, leaving a blazing trail as it encircles the luminescent symbol. The text settles into an arc upturned like a smile below the symbol, the two slogans forming a perfect circle, the whole thing seeming to burn brighter, brighter and brighter, searing through my retinas.

"*We finally know who we are and where we belong,*" she proclaims as the radiant Animus symbol quickly morphs to a peace symbol and then back, before vanishing altogether.

The lights come up slowly, giving our eyes ample time to readjust. Then a tall well-built man strolls out from behind a formal side draping. He strolls across the stage like he's walking into a room full of his closest and most trusted friends. He looks to be in his mid-thirties with dark wavy brown hair, and he's not wearing a robe or cape like everyone else. He's relaxed in blue jeans and a button-down shirt just like Roman's, only black.

"Who is that?" I whisper.

"That's Jakob," Roman whispers back, as the enormous assembly is utterly silent. "He's like the president of Antiquus, only we don't call him that. We just call him Jakob. He keeps things really informal. He's the one who made me a Sage—officially, anyway. He fought for me to be allowed to stay here."

My eyes are fixed on Jakob as he drinks from a bottle of water in his hand and paces about, seeming to gather his thoughts. It's odd to sit here, knowing that without him, this man I've never met before, Roman wouldn't be here in Antiquus, and without Roman caring for me, I wouldn't be here either. Roman would be in Primitus, where I can only imagine what Shamus would do to him, and I would surely be dead. It's only natural that I should be very grateful to him, a feeling I decide to put on reserve until I find out why he did it.

"Alan Turing," he begins, his voice smooth, likable, brimming with confidence, "considered to be the father of modern computer science, not a likable guy particularly, but undisputed in his genius. Often deterred but never daunted in his visionary quest to create something no one else could even conceive of in the late 1940s, the first universal computing machine. With this first computer, roughly the size of a semi-truck, he was able to crack the Germans' enigma codes, which became the crucial advantage in the Allies winning the war. The knowledge he was able to access was a very powerful thing."

His tone turns grave. "As far as some people were concerned, the power of this knowledge was dangerous, and should even be forbidden, for what it could do to this world—how a small handful of people might have the ability to completely reshape it.

"Turing died on June 7, 1954. Then, just a few short months later, on February 24, 1955, Steven Paul Jobs was born into this world and picked up right where Turning left off."

Jakob pauses, a curious look on his face. "Could it be? You might wonder. Was Turing reincarnated as Jobs?" He reaches into his pocket and pulls out an iPhone, marveling at the device in his hand. "The soul that was once Alan Turing accomplished so much, but I don't think he was done, not even close ... he wasn't much older than me when he died. So what happened to him, the young man who possessed this powerful *forbidden knowledge*? He was poisoned. Bit into a cyanide-laced apple." He holds up the back of his phone, showing us the familiar logo, an apple with a bite taken out of it. One or two people in the audience gasp at the coincidence.

"And the apple from the tree of knowledge strikes again," he quips to scattered laughter. "I tell you that amazing true story not just to enthrall and entertain you but because it's so exciting to know, for the first time in human history, what happens when we die. That reincarnation has been proven real. Think about that," he marvels.

"And I'm also thrilled to announce that we're working on brand-new devices for everyone. Well, the Sages are working, I should say. Aside from that, I'm sure you're all wondering why we're here. What's the reason for this unscheduled conclave? I'll get to all that in a minute, but I will tell you it's good; it's very good news."

There's a slight murmuring from the crowd, heads all turning as everyone quietly speculates to one another about what the good news could be. Everyone, that is, except a few people in the very front rows whose lack of movement catches my attention. Perhaps they already know.

"First I want to talk about what we knew—that we were living in a world on the verge of collapse." Jakob looks squarely out into the crowd. "I knew it," he admits, a mix of guilt and humility in his words. "We all knew that. We *felt* it, right? Long before the events, before the Unthinkable, we sensed it, didn't we?"

He nods, and most every head I can see slowly nods back. I even find myself nodding, though I'm not sure whether it's to blend in or because I agree with him.

"After the year 2000 began, I don't know, but there was this steady drum beat. Then after we all made it through December 21, 2012—" He waves his hands sarcastically about all the predictions of doom on that day, getting a chuckle from the crowd, "it suddenly began to feel as if it was only a matter of when, didn't it? A matter of *how* it was going to happen, of what was going to take us down. World War III, cyber terrorism, biological weapons, nukes, super storms, religious and political unrest … you name it, and it was threatening our civilization on a global scale. We knew what course we were on, and we knew that course was accelerating; we saw signs of that everywhere. For the first time in human history our demise was imminent; it was guaranteed. We could feel in our bones that we were on borrowed time. Couldn't we? I know I could. And yet …"

He pauses, seeming to grapple with what he's about to say. "What did we do? Did we fix it, work together, resolve the conflicts, stabilize our societies? Did we even try? Did we prepare, somehow, for this imminent end we all saw coming?" He pauses, and we answer with our silence.

"I struggled with that," he admits. "We were doing nothing. For all those years, with all those resources, everything at our fingertips, a pit of knowing in my stomach … What was our plan, as Americans? Why didn't we come together somehow to fortify ourselves against this impending collapse we all admit we were anticipating? I was beating myself up pretty badly until I realized why we hadn't—my proverbial light bulb moment."

He looks out into our faces. As his eyes sweep through our section, I try to subtly lean behind Roman. "Because deep inside somewhere, we did not want our current societies to survive," he declares, just as his eyes near mine.

My heart flies up in my chest. If he sees me, will he call me out, right here in front of everyone, for not sitting where I'm supposed to and God only knows what else? But to my relief, after a beat, he looks right past me and goes on.

"As many of you are probably aware, imprinted within us all is a record. This record isn't in your DNA. It's not like the Animus structure's record of your soul's lives. This record is within your soul itself. It's an etheric warehouse of sorts and contains everything that has occurred within the whole of the universe, every thought, feeling, emotion, and event, and it holds a complete set of information regarding all possibilities for the future."

I know this to be true. Cian had discussed it with me at length from the time I was very young. In fact, the vibration that Cian used to perform his duties as the waker came directly from these records.

"They are called the Akashic Records," Jakob continues, moving his gaze back toward me. Roman squeezes my hand as Jakob squints his eyes and tilts his head, looking straight in my direction. A subtle smile comes over him. Then he looks away and goes on:

"I now believe that we intentionally made no effort to preserve our way of life. You could even argue we helped to destroy it, unconsciously, of course. We actively weakened our own society. We began seeing only our differences with our neighbors and allowing our divisions to reach a genuine rage because, deep within our souls, we knew the time had come for us to evolve into something new. We even knew that there was something much better already waiting for us."

I glance at Roman, wondering if he knows what's coming next. He shrugs.

"We are here today to take a vote. Antiquus is a democracy, and today we make that official. Today we will vote whether or not to enact something that was set forth in 1776 by three of the Founding Fathers of the United States: Thomas Jefferson, John Adams, and James Monroe. These men knew in their bones what no one else wanted to accept—that we'd destroy ourselves from the inside out. That this first attempt at these ideals of theirs, life, liberty, and the pursuit of happiness was just that—a beta test, if you will. They knew that one day, on the continent of North America, things would fall into an unrecoverable calamity. Adversity, that as a community, we would never grow strong enough to handle. They planned an elaborate 'backup' system—that's what they called it at the time anyway, just a backup system. They preconceived and preconstructed all of this, with only the three of them knowing that it was our destiny all along—it was always in the stars, that Canada and Mexico and the United States would become one—*Aurora*."

"Aurora," he repeats, wistfully. "Doesn't it almost sound familiar?"

Aurora is Latin for "dawn" or "new beginning." Our Year Zero.

"Aurora will be a true democracy, where the citizens finally vote on the laws. America was not a democracy. It was a republic; elected leaders held the power to make the laws. In their hearts Jefferson, Adams, and Monroe knew we were supposed to be going even further, to put complete trust and faith in the people to govern themselves fully. Funny isn't it, how Americans always thought we lived in a democracy?

"Those Akashic Records are a beguiling thing. It's what I find most exciting of all. That this was the *full* plan all along. And in our souls we knew that two governing sister cities, Antiquus and Primitus, would someday replace the one corrupt power center of Washington and the two parties of American government. Those political identities were just a precursor to our ultimate destiny, becoming *Antiquuans* and *Primitans*, a global peace partnership that has united the whole world for the first time."

He starts clapping to signal how excited we should feel about this new world, under one global umbrella of peace. The crowd quickly joins in a rousing round of applause. "We are all one," he cheers, pumping his fist in the air as a few people hoot and holler in support.

"Sometimes I lie awake and wonder," he continues after the applause begins to die down, "how did they foresee the tsunami? How on Earth did they foresee Animus all the way back then? How did they know it would be discovered so long before it happened? Then I spend a day hanging out with the Sages, and I know." This earns him a flattered chuckle from the Sage section. "All right, that was your civics lesson for the day," he jokes with an easy charm, and I realize suddenly how *completely* I'd been listening—in a state of utter suggestibility. Not deciding whether I thought any of that was true or false, just believing it.

I glance around. Everyone has the same vacant focused stare, transfixed by Jakob and his enchanting stories, even Roman.

"Last thing is a history lesson. It's a good one," he smiles before taking a big sip of water from the bottle still in his hands. "Did you know that in the United States our *third* president, Thomas Jefferson, would die on July 4th, the date of America's independence, a date he was responsible for choosing. Coincidence? And that three of the Founding Fathers would end up dying on that very day. Three—" he repeats, holding up three fingers as a huge flag unfurls from the ceiling, right next to the one Roman called mine. Another gold flag, this one with three white stars across the center, then a triple tau within a triangle above the stars.

All enclosed within a circle, along with the word "Aurora." The triple tau ... *the emblem of Mercury ... the God's messenger ...* I start to recall, knowing there's more—

"That these three would each die on that historic day," Jakob's voice rises into my mind, derailing my train of thought, "I believe was a *message* from ... beyond—"

The word "message" catches my attention, bringing me back to myself and to my own thoughts ... *message ... messenger ... Mercury ...*

"That the death of America as we knew it would be the real birthday of the one world that these three visionaries saw. Three stars—" he points to the flag as we all stare at it— "for the three countries of North America, now one, and the three Founding Fathers who planned all of this for you—Aurora the *true* democracy ... Aurora, the true beginning ... Aurora, the dawn," he declares, a benediction, a consecration. With the rising anthem, already both familiar and comforting, even to me, everyone stands in unison. We're moved, *collectively.* Whether it's by the spirit of the Founding Fathers, by our baked-in fears, by suggestion, hypnosis, or brainwashing, or by our ultimate lack of other options, it doesn't really matter. The pomp and circumstance feels good. It's the feeling of strength in numbers, of unity. Peace and order. Like being cradled in a giant hand, out of reach of danger—invincible even. Most of all it's the feeling that it's what *we* have chosen.

Looking up at both flags, I shift my focus to the one Roman said was mine. It's the exact same golden color as the Aurora flag beside it—and the exact same size, much bigger than the flags of the other three collectives. One word is emblazed across the top in a pearlescent white thread: ZODIAC.

The strange symbol below the word seems to be made up of several different ancient symbols, one of which I note right away is the *ankh*, the ancient Egyptian symbol for life. Unlike the other flags, there are no descriptive words below the symbol. Then my eyes dart down to the tall white-tufted chair trimmed in gold, my chair. It stands alone near the center of the enormous grand hall.

How has all of this happened so quickly? It seems impossible, and I feel my stomach drop out, like I've suddenly woken up to discover we're not safe at all, that we're all on a rollercoaster that's careening off its track.

After the last notes of our new national anthem play, Jakob waves both his hands downward, and we all sit.

"Now I want to know what each and every one of you thinks, and of course we are going to vote on all of this … is this what *we* want? Is it how *we* see our future? But first, there is one more thing we must consider."

He walks toward the Sage section. "Orias, how many are left?" he asks an older man seated in the front row of Sages.

Orias stands up, a short old man, hands resting in a gentle clasp behind his green cape. He reminds me so much of Cian.

"As of last year, the total world population was just over 7.4 billion." Orias pauses, then takes a deep breath. "The total population of North America before the events, before the unthinkable, before the dark days that followed, was four hundred eighty-six million two hundred thirty-four thousand, five hundred four. Today, just before this conclave, I saw the total populations of both the world and of North America—" Orias stops. Taking another deep inhale, he appears to be struggling to remain calm.

"One of the many benefits of having Sages around," Jakob remarks to the crowd. "All right, what are the numbers, Orias?"

Orias opens his mouth but stops again, and Jakob puts his hand on the old man's shoulder. "It's okay," Jakob says, "things are going to be okay."

Finally, Orias clears his throat. "Total world population has fallen to just below 500 million."

His announcement sends an audible wave of shock through the mass of people, then the rustle of anxious murmuring.

"In North America, where of course the tsunami struck, claiming, all told, over 100 million lives. And where—" Orias breaks off, unable to go on. He begins to weep, his hunched shoulders convulsing as Jakob pulls him into an embrace.

They share a quiet private exchange.

"Orias and his wife, Helen—" Jakob motions to an older woman with long silver hair across the way, seated in the first row of Dragons. She stands reluctantly and walks toward them, her long black robe billowing behind her. When she reaches her husband, they embrace.

"Like so many of you, Helen and Orias have lost their entire family," Jakob tells us. Seeing the pain on the couple's faces, I feel a lump in my throat. I glance around. Most people watch with tears streaming down from their eyes.

"These are dark times," Orias mumbles. Jakob nods, urging him on. "On our continent ... we've lost the largest percentage," he continues, his voice unsteady. "Just over 17.5 million ... that's, that's all that's left."

Silence always seems louder the more people it comes from, and the silence after this grave announcement is deafening.

"Can anyone confirm this?" Jakob asks into the stunned crowd. "I don't make a habit of doubting Orias, mind you,

I'm just not able to look into bowls of water and see numbers and mystical things like the Sages. The visions I get are a little different than that." He glances around briefly, and then his eyes fall right on me.

Fiorella stands up, donning a black robe. I couldn't be happier to see her, to know that she's here and that she's safe. Even across this vast space, just looking at her brings me a rush of comfort. I wonder how she's handling the loss of Maricielo.

"Since we arrived here, I'm told that my daughter Zeppelin has been ... refining her gifts," she says, looking into the Sage section with a nod. About twenty-five rows above us, Zeppelin stands, fidgeting, nervous. After a brief moment of quiet, Fiorella gives her another nod and a stern raise of her brows.

"It's true, I saw the same number," Zeppelin says.

Zee clearly dislikes the spotlight and the attention, that's easy to see. But whether or not she's being truthful, that's much harder to tell. Something is making me suspect that she isn't.

With a gesture from Jakob, the lights dim slightly and another hologram projects in the air above us—the words "Total North American Population." Jakob asks Zee for the exact number.

"Seventeen million," she says slowly, "seven hundred

sixty-one thousand, seven hundred seventy-six." The number appears in the hologram, Orias nodding in agreement as it does.

Jakob paces as he stares at the numbers with his hands resting on his hips. Then Orias points toward the hologram. His finger is wagging; it's clear he is trying to say something but nothing is coming out of his mouth. It's like he's seeing a ghost.

"The commas," he says to Jakob finally, his voice shaking. "The commas—take them out!"

"Remove the commas, please!" Jakob orders, and they dissolve away. "Remove the spaces, please," he adds, and the eight digits come together. Orias is waving his finger at the number but simply cannot speak.

"Put a space between the six and the one, please," Jakob says, and an audible gasp escapes from the crowd.

The number now reads: 1776 1776.

SEVEN

— ✦ —

It's not hard to guess how the vote went after that.

After what couldn't be anything other than a supernatural nudge from somewhere beyond, with the strange feeling of making a choice where there really was no choice at all, the historic Founding of Aurora happened right before our eyes. A unanimous vote, all yea and no nay, our first civic duty as Antiquuans was now officially in the books. And after a very short speech from Jakob, which I noted he read from a piece of paper, informing us that a similar vote will take place in the coming days in Primitus. He then anointed us as everything the human race had been working toward: Antiquuans, the old souls, the voices of reason. And then the conclave was concluded.

The six men I noticed, two from each collective, who didn't appear to be wondering what the big announcement was going to be, now stand around Jakob and are talking quietly with him. I don't know the men in white and black but getting a better look at the two green-robed men, I recognize exactly who they are—Karl Alastair, the creator of Animus, the evil genius who launched the smear campaign against me based on my IN number, and Marcus Joplin, the religious scholar who was consistently ranting on TV throughout the events, the unthinkable and everything after, pushing the biblical narrative of apocalypse well beyond any reasonable or rational limits.

"What's that about?" I ask Roman, motioning toward Jakob and the men gathered around him as everyone near us stands up to leave.

"High Commission," he says. "The top *advisers* from each collective," he explains with a raise of his eyebrows, and we exchange a worried look. "We should try to sneak out before anyone spots us," he whispers.

I glance around. Fiorella and Zee both are too far away for me to get to without drawing attention to myself. A bottleneck has already begun to form at the one exit, which we are several rows up and a section away from. I fidget as I stand behind Roman, waiting for our row to begin clearing into the aisle. The question of where he and I should go once we get out of here is buzzing around like an aggressive gnat in my mind.

"This won't take long; it never does." Roman smiles, turning his body toward mine, trying to reassure me. "You probably need to process all this. Someplace quiet …" he says, looking down at my face with tender eyes. I marvel at how he's always so aware of my needs, as he seems to be going through a laundry list of places in his head where we might go, where I'll be able to sort through my thoughts.

Standing so close, breathing him in, watching him think—trying to come up with what the best thing for me might be—one place suddenly comes to mind.

"Let's go to my bedroom," I suggest just as the daring thought flares in my brain like a rogue firework.

It was a bold thing to say. I realize that, after the fact. And it certainly seems to catch Roman off guard, by the look of surprise on his face anyway, for what it sounds like I'm implying. But the truth is, he's all I want right now— nothing and no one else. I just want to be alone with him somewhere very private. There's no script in my head for what will happen after that.

He studies me, trying to look into my soul. His breathing becomes heavier, and the air between us changes, like a drop in the barometric pressure.

"Are you sure?" he asks, unequivocal about what he's just heard me say that I want. And for a moment, I freeze. There's absolutely nothing boyish about Roman anymore;

over the last six weeks, he's turned into a man. There's nothing hidden; there are no games. It's a very good question he's asking, loaded with important things, the things I am implying to him, things that send my stomach up into my heart. Things that make my palms sweat and my insides ignite. Do I want to be with him? It certainly sounds like that's what I was saying, but am I sure? I search my soul for a brief second and realize very quickly, that when it comes to Roman, there's absolutely nothing I'm unsure about.

"I am," I say quite freely, feeling him sense how certain I am and watching how it changes him. How his bright, sparkling eyes, which have been searching mine, go from intense and worried to glad and relaxed. His gaze moves slowly to my forehead, and he leans down toward me until I feel his smooth lips lightly brushing against my head, and his body pressing softly into mine. He exhales, a tiny burst of his sweet breath onto my skin, like a gift, a bit of himself shared with me, flaring up the blaze in my core he's been stoking all day. Closing my eyes to focus all my senses on this moment, he presses a warm sensual kiss into the very center of my forehead, his pursed lips softly lingering there. I grab onto his arms, gripping on tight where his biceps meet his elbows, wanting this moment to never end.

When after a heavenly few seconds of feeling his body

pressed against mine and breathing him in, it does finally end. He looks down at me. First into my eyes, then at every part of my face, like he's memorizing each detail, searing this me and this moment into his memory.

"I love you, Eve," he confesses, pouring the words into me, straight from his soul into mine. "I have been hopelessly in love with you," he whispers into my ear, "every lifetime I have ever lived—and madly in love, beside myself with love, since the moment I saw you in this one."

As we head for the exit I notice the way my hand rests in his. It's so natural. It feels like something we've been doing for centuries. I also feel certain about where we're heading, more certain than anything I've felt in a very long time, or ever. We're trying our best to dissolve into the mass exodus, still needing to blend in while also wanting to burst through it, trying to get where we've decided to go as quickly as we can.

He glances back at me every few minutes, rolling his eyes at the hordes of people leisurely milling together, and we start quietly laughing at ourselves. At how impatient we are to get out of here.

As we finally approach the doors, Roman's warm hand locks tighter onto mine, squeezing it gently. Then I feel another hand, a heavy one, as it lands on my shoulder.

"Eve." I turn around to see Jakob standing before us. Looking relaxed, holding a fresh bottle of water, he takes me in. Up close, his commanding presence radiates even more strongly than it does when he eloquently holds tens of thousands of people in the palm of his hand. He's also larger than I thought, taller with a broader chest and shoulders—a strikingly similar height and build to Roman. There's something inhumanly magnetic about him, a strange gravity into his blue-eyed gaze, a cool congenial smile exuding utter trustworthiness—both of which I find instantly alarming.

"Eve, you look well," he remarks, as if he knows me, yet he's seeming caught off guard by my condition. "You look *very* well," he marvels, studying me, and I feel Roman inching ever so slightly closer into my side.

"Thank you," I say. Then the three of us fall into an awkward silence.

"I'm so sorry—allow me to introduce myself." Jakob holds out his hand.

He's rolled up both his sleeves to his elbows since the conclave, and I look down at his IN tattoo, CMXCIX, the Roman numeral for 999, stamped across his forearm in bold dark black ink.

"Dragon soul. Nothing even close to you, of course," he says with gravity in his voice and humility in his gaze, both of which throw me off kilter. "But you haven't got your tattoo yet."

I rub my right forearm. "Uh, no," I say, feeling almost guilty.

"Your secret's safe with me," he whispers, smiling at both Roman and me, and I'm suddenly reminded of what he did for us, the secret reason why Roman is even here.

"Jakob, right," I say, and we shake hands. Mine feels very small in his in a way I don't particularly like, in a way that makes *me* feel small, breakable.

"Yes, I'm sorry," he apologizes again—his second apology in roughly twenty seconds—which I note has the effect of making him seem instantly human, genuinely humble, and incredibly gracious. It also makes something finally click in my brain—suspicion.

"It's amazing, isn't it?" he says. "Everything that's happened here today, don't you think? It's truly incredible." He answers his own question, which seems like a telling quality. What if I say no? That I don't think it is amazing or incredible. What will happen then?

"Eve, is everything all right?" he asks.

"Fine," I lie. It's a bit soon for hurling accusation of malice and mind games.

"Good, I'm glad to hear it. I want you to be *very* happy here. You can always come to me, privately, if something's ever bothering you." His words practically ooze with sincerity, but I catch something else glimmering in his eye, a dark spot he can't hide where a hint of falseness lies.

Cian often talked about separating the truth from the illusions. He told me something that comes to mind now, as I stand before Jakob: *The people who can fake sincerity the best are the ones that ought to worry you most. They are the false prophets.*

"Anything at all, that's what I'm here for," Jakob says. "You just let me know."

"All right," I agree.

"Good," he says, sounding quite satisfied. "Now, Eve, there are some people who couldn't be here today but who are very eager to meet you," he adds in a more hushed voice, looking around at the crowds who continue to file past us. I get the hint—that this meeting isn't something for everyone, that these are "different" people than the ones all around us.

"Roman, would you mind terribly if I steal her away for just a short time?" He rushes out, doing a sloppy job disguising the patronizing edge to his friendly tone.

Maybe it's because I'm already suspicious of Jakob, or maybe it's because this is one detour I really don't want to take right now, or maybe I just don't like seeing Roman disrespected, but at that moment something inside me cracks.

"You know what?" I interrupt before Roman has a chance to answer. "There *is* something that's beginning to bother me here."

"Of course. Yes, what is it?" Jakob asks, overly eager.

I lean toward Jakob, and he drops his head in to listen, his expression one of an executive problem solver, ready troubleshooter.

"The illusion of choice," I whisper slowly, right into his ear.

Then I step back and watch his face reveal that he knows exactly what I'm talking about. That he's caught. No one else may notice, but I do. "Sit any place you'd like," provided it's in the section that has your name on it, "vote yes or no" on a matter with one *very clear* correct answer, a conclave that "isn't mandatory," yet no one seemed to believe it was all right to skip. The insulting illusion of a choice he just attempted to belittle Roman with.

"I think I'd be much more comfortable if Roman could join us," I say after a long awkward pause, dramatically looking around at the people who continue to file past, just as he did. "Jakob, would you mind terribly." It's not a question.

Jakob's friendly face has gone blank, utterly taken aback both by the request and by me—like he doesn't know quite what he's going to do with either.

"Of course," he forces out through a stiff jaw, a strained little smile.

The tunnel system that exists below Antiquus is like a vast network of arteries, a never-ending maze of interconnected passageways that can withstand virtually anything man or nature could ever dish out, built over two hundred years ago—*allegedly* (eye roll). And after only just a few minutes of Roman and I following behind Jakob through the gargantuan winding stone passages, two things had happened: I was already completely turned around, and Jakob was inviting us into his grand illusion once again.

"It is *impressive*," he remarks definitively, "all of this created centuries ago," marveling at the spectacular structure, giving a double pound of his fist on the smooth granite wall as we walk past to prove how unyielding it is, looking up to where it curves in to form the rounded ceiling fifteen or twenty feet overhead. Out of basic human instinct, Roman and I follow his gaze, looking to the ceiling as well. And as I stare up at these indestructible catacombs, trying to conceive of how they were constructed, I'm annoyed to hear the word "impressive" hypnotically looping through my mind. He not only wants to tell us what to do, where to sit, and how to vote, he wants to tell us what to think.

Staring at the back of him, I notice his freshly cut hair,

not a single strand out of place, the creases of his flawlessly pressed tucked-in shirt, his black loafers shined to a mirror finish, the way his hands are balled into tight fists at the ends of his swinging arms—this guy's a real control freak. The jeans say casual and the rolled-up sleeves say relaxed, a president who prefers he be on a first-name basis with everyone ... all I see are conscious attempts to lower people's defenses.

Jakob points down a large corridor, which leads to a web of corridors that spider off from it like fingers. "One of our more recently filled food storage wings," he boasts, as if he did the work himself.

I turn my head to get a look as we walk past. The huge block of passageways, each filled with unending rows of white five-gallon containers, go on and on, far beyond where I can see, housing thousands upon thousands upon thousands *upon thousands* of containers.

"Wow," I remark on the staggering amount of food, the magnitude of it all, and look up to see Jakob smiling back at me.

"Impressive, wouldn't you say?" he asks, cueing up the stupid word he's trying to implant in my brain. Practically begging me to say it. So, of course, I decide to say nothing. Screw him and his stupid mind games. I respond with a long unblinking silence, a decidedly unimpressed glare that rapidly makes everyone uncomfortable but me.

"Yes," Roman says. "Obviously. It's very impressive. Of course, right?" he says, eyeing me. Once Jakob's back is to us, Roman cautions me with a look. He knows what I'm trying to do. To extinguish Jakob's power like a blanket thrown on a fire, even if it's just for a minute. And he's warning me not to get ahead of myself, reminding me with a subtle raise of his eyebrows that Jakob holds Roman's fate in his hands.

He's right, I realize. I'm going to have to learn to play along.

We descend even deeper to where the aquifers run, rivers of crystal-blue water flowing through large square-shaped channels of smooth rock, which Jakob says are filled with centuries of rain and snow melt and connect to hundreds of natural underground springs, an inexhaustible water source, then finally to where this particular tunnel ends. A large wooden double door, not unlike the ones to my bedroom, looms before us.

Jakob turns around. His tone is suddenly stern, even threatening.

"What you are about to see is never to be discussed," he warns us. "Anything you hear on the other side of these doors is never to be mentioned to anyone under any circumstance.

Am I making myself clear?" he asks, eyeing Roman in particular.

We both nod, and the doors begin to open inward, moving slowly away from us as we stand motionless before them.

Roman and I follow Jakob into a magnificent library of sorts, a remarkable room, like I'd imagine the private study of Leonardo da Vinci. There are six walls; each topped with stone-carved grand arches that curve inward where the ceiling begins, all leading to a single point in the middle. Dripping down from the center of the dome in seven stacked tiers, like an upside down wedding cake frosted in diamonds, is a massive bronze and crystal chandelier that anoints the whole space with a warm, luxurious glow. Each wall is filled with a dizzying number of wooden shelves running all the way up to the high ceiling and stacked top to bottom with leather-bound books in every conceivable color. Dark wooden ladders provide access to every last book.

When my eyes finally drift downward, I see six recessed caves, like large cubbies carved out of limestone, one at the foot of each wall. Inside each well-lit spacious nook is a claw-footed mahogany desk. Their surfaces are decorated with maps, sketches, laboratory beakers, microscopes, plants and flowers being dissected and examined, and unending stacks of books.

The six people who stand in the very center of the large hexagon are just as much of a spectacle as the astonishing room they occupy. Skull and Bones, Freemasons, Illuminati ... these are all fronts, I realize, figments of people's imaginations, or merely tendrils of the real power center before me now.

Ansel stands among the three men and three women before us, all of them wearing long flowing capes: two black, two green, and two white. But these capes are much heavier than those I saw at the conclave, more like cloaks with longer heavier hoods and draping velvet fabric, and each is clasped at the front with a thick gold pin. It's hard to make out what it is from a distance, but I know it has some kind of eye in the center.

"These are six of the twelve total members of the Aion Dorea, a very special group of clandestine, faithful servants of humanity," Jakob tells us. "The other six members— Bael, Kazaar, Claudius, Druscilla, Thea, and Kali—are currently residing in Primitus. And, I'm told, for the foreseeable future.

"Hello Eve," says Ansel's familiar voice. He smiles and nods, looking happy to see me. Relieved. One of the last times I saw Ansel, he was telling me the meaning and mission of the Aion Dorea, which he too claimed to be "faithful servants of humanity," despite the actual Greek translation of the words being, roughly, "the gift of eternal time." This occurred right before Pope Gelasius II warned me to look out for those offering a "gift," and right before the shocking and brutal murder of my grandfather. So needless to say, I'm feeling a bit uneasy about the six cloaked individuals before me.

"Ansel, who you know," Jakob starts the introductions as the caped figures step toward us.

"Sourial," he says, motioning to the red-haired woman whose stunning face I've seen and whose soothing voice I've heard but who I've never actually met. She's wearing a long dark green cloak that matches the deep pine color of her eyes.

"Rasuil." A dark-haired middle-aged man, Latin American perhaps. He bears a strong resemblance to Maricielo and wears a black cloak.

"Pythagoras." A much older man with stark white hair, bushy white eyebrows, and kind brown eyes that twinkle behind thick glasses wearing a green cloak.

"And this is Clio," Jakob says of the smaller one in the white cloak. She looks to be around my age, maybe a bit younger, sixteen perhaps, a tiny girl with long blond hair and stunning eyes, a bright sparkling pale blue, like they're made from the pristine water of the aquifers, with rings of gold around her pupils.

"And last," Jakob motions to the tall, beautiful, dark-haired woman in a white robe standing next to Clio, "this is Bronwyn." Her smile lights up her twinkling green eyes, which bear a stunning resemblance to mine and to Roman's. *If I had a mother*, I think as I study her, *this is exactly how I imagine she would look.*

Now that they're standing closer to us, I can see that the outer circle of the pins they're wearing is actually an ouroboros—a serpent devouring its own tail, a symbol that first appeared in ancient Egypt and India. It means the eternal return of something existing from the beginning of time with such force it cannot be extinguished. Within that is the eye shape, the Eye of Horus—an ancient Egyptian symbol of protection and royal power. At the very center is a *mitsudomoe*—a Japanese symbol from the Shinto religion for man, earth, and sky, representing their god of war.

"Eve," Pythagoras says, "we are all so very sorry about the loss of your grandfather. We extend our deepest condolences, and we mourn him with you."

"Thank you," I say, feeling a small splash of relief to share the burden of his loss with others who knew and loved him.

"A collapsed windpipe," Ansel says, eyeing me, "is a very difficult way to imagine a loved one leaving this world. I want you to know that the medical staff was able to determine, forensically, that he didn't suffer long, if at all. His death was almost instant. I hope this will bring you a small measure of comfort. I know it did for me."

"Thank you," I say, unsure of why Ansel is lying about the cause of Cian's death. It probably has something to do with protecting Shamus, but now is not the time to try to find out.

"Clio has recently joined us in his place," Bronwyn says, her voice like a dark calm sea. I look at the young girl in the flowing white robe, her face serene and beautiful. She's like an angel who decided to take a human form.

"So ... it's true then," I start cautiously. "Cian was a part of this ... Aion Dorea," I say, still feeling unsure that he actually was, and not knowing what they truly are. "I have to say, I find it odd that he never mentioned anything about it to me," I add with a voice that's beginning to shake. "He didn't keep things from me. He told me everything."

"This is something he couldn't reveal, Eve, not to anyone, not even to you," Ansel says. "Our existence has never been acknowledged—*and never can be*," he emphasizes, a warning glare directed particularly toward me. "But I assure you, it's true. Cian was long a key member of the Aion Dorea, just as I told you on the night you first arrived here," he adds, as if he's positively baffled that I would ever doubt anything he tells me.

Besides having a bizarre talent for quickly pissing me off, I always get the strange feeling that Ansel's making the case for his own trustworthiness, which, of course, always strikes me as utterly suspicious.

I'm already unnerved that he lied about how Cian died, not to mention that the very last time I saw him, just before my jaunt to the dark side, he clearly had lizard eyes and reptilian skin. Though I'm not sure that the things people see mere seconds before their mind is flung to Timbuktu can be completely reliable. But still, combining all that with the high likelihood he knew—based on when Phoenix said the phone in my house started ringing again on the night of the tsunami—that Shamus wasn't missing at all but was actually in the house when I arrived home, that it's reasonable to assume he even spoke with him, and the fact that he didn't tell me that, all shifts Ansel into the column of "suspected alliance with my evil brother."

"So, what changed, huh?" I snap at Ansel. "Why am I suddenly allowed to know about the Aion Dorea? Especially when it's obvious what a highly protected secret all this is …"

But it's not Ansel who answers. "In accordance with your grandfather's wishes," Pythagoras says, handing me a document. "For you. Evelyn Sophia O'Cleirigh, your grandfather's will."

I take the rolled-up parchment and pull it open just a bit. In formal calligraphy it reads "The Last Will and Testament of Cian Malachi O'Cleirigh, exclusive property of his sole heir: Evelyn Sophia O'Cleirigh."

Cian had a will? My middle name is Sophia? Cian's middle name was Malachi? I'm his sole heir? What about Shamus?

"Cian asked, should his passing become imminent, that you be made aware of our existence," Pythagoras says. "And so Ansel told you as quickly as possible. Cian felt very strongly you needed to know about us … and about many other things as well." He nods toward the will in my hands. "It's for you to read, and you alone."

"Thank you. I'll look it over," I mumble, trying to imagine what it will say.

"Eve," Clio says to me, a wisdom in her voice far beyond

her years. "It's an honor for me to meet you finally." Her crystal eyes sparkle with a strange transcendent innocence, reminding me of Jude's.

"Clio has been studying your grandfather her whole life, and so studying your life as well. She knows everything about you," Pythagoras says, giving me a look like I may want to ask her some questions at some point. "She was born to fill Cian's spot ... when that time came." I see in his face that there are still moments when he struggles to accept Cian's death.

"Do you have the same gift he had?" I ask Clio, hopeful.

"Oh, no," she says. "I'm afraid I don't."

"There has always been one," Ansel says, "who's had *the gift,* as it's been known to us. Since around 30 BC, one member of the Aion Dorea was always here to assist the hand of fate, as it were. That is, until now."

"Since the fall of Egypt?" I ask, intrigued, wondering about the connection. "But never before that?"

Bronwyn casts her face slightly downward, trying to conceal a smile.

"Your grandfather wasn't exaggerating about you, was he?" Pythagoras marvels. "You get right to the heart of things, don't you?"

"That, my dear, is a *very* good question," Bronwyn says, seeming eager to discuss it with me.

"A good question, yes, but one for another time," Ansel says to Pythagoras. "We knew after Cian was gone," he continues somberly, "that we would be entering a new era, a period where there would be no waker. Humanity is completely on its own."

"The coordinates are set; we're just charting a course now," Pythagoras says.

A heavy mood blankets the room.

"The dawn of new a beginning," Jakob chimes in, his enthusiasm jarring against the reverence of the moment. Sourial and Rasuil nod in agreement with him, as if they are eagerly awaiting the start of this fated new era. And thus eagerly awaiting my grandfather's exit from this world. *Even, perhaps, just as eager as Shamus was to be rid of Cian*, I think to myself, eyeing them all, quietly scooting Rasuil and Sourial into the column with Ansel in my mind.

Ansel slowly opens the front of his cape, revealing a small golden urn in the crook of his elbow. He holds it out to me—an urn, I realize, filled with the remains of my grandfather.

I take it without a word.

"There will be a service in the morning," he says, "just before sunrise, where his life will be celebrated. Your grandfather was a Mountain soul. So it will be held on the

Subterranean level where the Mountain souls live, in the heart of their most sacred temple."

"We cannot attend, of course," Bronwyn says, "but we will join you in spirit." She takes a step toward me, and I begin to feel an electric current running along my spine, as if an invisible sphere of life surrounds her. And though I haven't noticed it before, in one of her hands she's holding a beautiful white lily on a long green stem.

"You may find it … difficult to sleep—there's a very powerful full moon tonight," she says to me slowly, a deep wisdom in her eyes. "For you," she says, and with my hands occupied with Cian's ashes and his will, she gives the flower to Roman before stepping back to join the others.

We walk back in silence, Roman and I following behind Jakob. It will take almost a full hour to cover the ground back to where we started.

This time I don't look at any of the mysterious dark tunnels we pass. I don't marvel at the complexity of the aquifers. I just stare down at the ground, at my snow boots plodding forward step-by-step. Carrying me along. The ones Roman put beside my bed to save my feet from the frostbite I'd have surely given myself. The laces swinging about erratically, still untied. Just as they were this morning when I went outside to chop wood, utterly unaware of the world.

The tall rubber boots hang loose around my ankles, the reinforced tips of the brown laces ticking against the ground with each step.

I barely made it through my bedroom door this morning, and now I'm clutching Cian's ashes tightly in my arms. His entire body inside something the size of a coffee can. Humanity left to its own. Lies everywhere. The truth obscured, little more than an uncertain shimmer in the distance, all of which is going to make cracking the all-important code fairly impossible. Certainly well beyond metaphors of needles and haystacks, yet hardwired into my soul is the undeterred drive to accomplish it. I know I'll stop at nothing.

So I sink into a hopeless drowning feeling.

Not only that, I have a mammoth job to do, one that no reasonable person would think possible, and that I have no idea how I'm going to accomplish, but it's also beginning to seem like the fate of humanity is hanging in the balance. Not to mention my sneaking suspicion that who and what I'm up against are as formidable as they are mysterious, roving packs of wolves, most in sheep's clothing.

A sudden resurgence of abandonment squeezes my heart again.

Even after you think you've gotten past something, it can flare back up at any moment—detonate inside you without warning. It can be triggered at any second and by any number of things. And I've just been thrown a grenade, an explosion of unjustified resentment, a bottomless angry ache, that somehow Cian could have decided to stay alive, if he'd really wanted to. I know that feeling is nonsense, but that does nothing to quell the wretched sting once it starts seeping in. Beyond any kind of loneliness, abandonment carries a particular sensation of being taken out into space by the ones you love most and just left there, expelled into a hostile environment, a place where you have all but zero chance of surviving, but where you now have to stay and try to make a new home for yourself.

"But there's no food, water, or oxygen," you might say if anyone were listening. "This atmosphere isn't for humans; my skin will disintegrate from my bones ..." But no one cares. No one can even hear you.

You are alone.

The sole heir indeed. A fairly ironic title, I think, as I glance down at Cian's will in my hand. I begin quietly unrolling it as we walk.

Just until I'm able to read the first few lines:

Eve, if you're reading this, then I've left behind the physical form you're used to me inhabiting. You've also learned of the existence of the Aion Dorea. Now the time has come for you to know a few more things, two of which I have written below.

First, remember, I've simply woken up from a dream; fear not death.

And second, Shamus is not your brother.

EIGHT

———— ✦ ————

Frustration has been a running theme in my day.

Of the "few things" it is time for me to know, only those two are written down—death's not a big deal, and Shamus isn't my brother. No other "things" and no explanations. Though I'm not remotely able to comprehend what it says, it is for my eyes only, so I'm not allowed to talk about it.

Below that mind-numbing mess, in the remaining three lines of his will, Cian bequeaths me all his worldly possessions: one nightstand, the contents and whereabouts of which are unknown. And one financial fortune— literally, nearly three hundred million dollars, which I, of course, never imagined he possessed, all mine at a time when there are no banks to keep it in and no stores to spend it in, in a world where the American government has collapsed.

I guess it's the thought that counts. Or maybe it's a clue? Money was never the currency of this world—that's painfully obvious now—but I still don't know what is.

Roman hasn't even looked in my general direction since the second I began reading Cian's will. And now that I've rolled it back up, he doesn't ask about it either. Even during the long semi-awkward walk from where Jakob left us in the common area all the way back to my room. Instead, he comforts me with reassuring words when I cry to him for reasons I don't want to explain. Then he asks if I'd like him to carry the urn, which he correctly guesses is growing heavy.

"Switch," he suggests—the urn for the flower. But first he breathes in the scent of the beautiful long-stem lily, his eyes closed, before presenting it to me.

"Thank you," I say, and hold it to my nose. It smells lush, sensual even.

Roman wraps his arm around my shoulders as we continue on. "There are a few dresses hanging in your closet—pretty ones, and nice shoes too," he says with a smile, trying to put my mind at ease in case I had thought to wonder whether I'd be wearing this brown potato sack and messy snow boots to Cian's funeral in the morning.

"I didn't even know I had a closet." I'm not joking, not really, but my random remark makes Roman chuckle. Just a bit at first, then he tosses his head back and bursts into a hearty laugh, one that turns so uncontrollable it becomes contagious and infects me. All the stress, the emotions, and the ridiculous frustrations of the day seem to have made us as punchy as after a night without sleep.

We stand there in the empty hall, our mouths wide open, laughing like two stoners, Cian's ashes clutched tightly in Roman's hands.

"Wait, wait, wait … Did you even know your middle name was Sophia?" he asks, almost unable to get the words out. I double over, practically retching with laughter, my knees threatening to buckle underneath me as I grab my stomach to try to stop it from seizing.

"No, I didn't know," I say, then return to my hysterics. We must look like a couple of escaped mental patients, living happily in an alternate universe. I try to explain this thought to him but only manage to point at us and up and down the hall a few times.

"I could tell …" he says, "you didn't know your own name … by the look on your—" his words are swallowed up by his laughter, so he just points to his own face.

Our fit lasts a good five minutes. Then we start walking again, the last hundred feet or so to my room, and I think of how everything is better, more fun, with Roman by my side. What an amazing creature he is, somehow even more stunning on the inside than he is breathtaking on the outside. Thoughtful, loyal, and loving.

I look at Roman holding Cian's urn, walking so closely beside me, still smiling, his cheeks still wet with tears of laughter. In the dimly lit long corridor where the shadows of demons taunted me this morning, now it seems the fiery crimson light only burns to illuminate my soul mate. I know so much more about him now. Not just what I've learned today, but everything he's done for me over the past six weeks. His sense of honor and how much he truly loves me is almost incomprehensible. And yet he's showing me all the time while never looking for anything in return.

I'm sure he's curious about the will, but I know he'll never ask me. And how he steered me toward Jude because it was what he was supposed to do—for me, for reasons neither of us understand yet, no matter how excruciating it was. He's all honor, unselfish to the core. He's always clearing the path ahead—*and loving me*—because he is who he is.

"Hey," I say into the comfortable quiet we've been sharing as we walk.

"Yeah," he says, stopping in front of the doors to my room. We turn toward one another, and I wonder what he's thinking, whether we'll stay together as we'd planned to before. Or maybe Roman's just escorting me to my door. He might be asking himself the same question, but in a situation that anyone else would make incredibly awkward, Roman is nothing but relaxed.

I search deep into his lush green eyes, and clear as day, I see my own heart.

"I love you," I say, slowly, trying to emphasize each word with how much I truly mean it. He looks surprised. Like it isn't something he is expecting to hear.

"Not just, I loved you in other lifetimes and I remember how it felt, which I do," I say. "What I mean is I love *you* … here, now … I love everything about you, in this life and in this moment. And I always will," I say, feeling every wall and every circumstance that ever stood in between us dissolve to dust.

Looking up at his angular face and tousled hair, his sexy olive skin, my heart pounds. There's so much love and so much depth and so much desire between us, and we've never even kissed before.

He laces the fingers of his hand with mine, and for a second he just looks down into my eyes. My breath gets heavier as he lingers over me, searching for what I want. Then he finally leans in and presses his lips hard into mine, kissing me with the unearthly force of the love of every lifetime in his heart and with the hurricane of love he feels for me now. He makes my knees wobble. He grabs the front of my shirt and pulls me in tighter, and I fall toward him, his back landing hard against my door with a thud, the heat of our kissing rising fast.

His lips part, his tongue moves slowly into my mouth, and the electric current, the life force I felt earlier, surges through my nerves. Reaching behind his back, he fumbles for the handle. Then, wrapping his arm around my waist, he pulls me into my bedroom.

It's three in the morning.

Though we haven't slept at all, just as Bronwyn had predicted, I feel as if I am more awake than I've ever been in my entire life. I feel *life*, in fact. I can feel it coursing through me. I can feel everything, sense everything as I lay there, my naked body entwined with his. I feel the coolness of the air as it slips into my lungs, the warmth of my own body, the tiny hairs on my arms, the waves of energy emanating off Roman. And when he shifts to lie on his back, his head resting on my stomach, I can feel the very pulse of life in my low abdomen beating gently against him.

Cian's service will start in only a couple of hours. Roman and I have just finished showering in the spectacular marble steam shower that apparently exists within the luxurious grand suite that is my room. In which, as Roman has told me, there are several pale-colored dresses hanging inside a tall mahogany wardrobe, each of which is more beautiful than the next.

In fact, there are a lot of clothes—all pale earth tones, but they are nice. And perfume, jewelry, anything else I could ever want. There is also a cot, an unmade mess of sheets and blankets in a corner of the room, where Roman tells me he basically lived for the last six weeks.

Lying there, feeling every thread of the silky sheets beneath my bare skin, I comb my fingers through his thick, messy hair. My brain is drowning in the smell of him, a musky sweet vanilla mixed with the delicate scent of French lavender soap. I can even feel his body's vibration—maybe I'm just high from what we've been doing, from having him, fully, but I swear I can. It's like a sonic fingerprint, as unique as his body, mind, and soul. And I feel it changing, slowing down after having made love to me, finally, and slowing further every time my nails gently rake across his scalp.

The weight of him keeps increasing on me too as he sinks deeper, his head and shoulders falling farther and farther into me. I feel the tangle of our energies as they dance and merge, making something new.

I can feel energy, I realize.

I focus all my attention on it, on the difference between

his energy and mine, our perfect yin and yang, and watch it materialize before my eyes. The atoms of our energy visually manifest. Mine is sparkling and deep red, particles of matter that swirl around like a powerful storm, a glittering tornado, dangerously inviting. And his are a brilliant white, strong, vibrant, and steady like waves of pure light lapping rhythmically onto warm sumptuous white beach sand. The more I caress his head, the more he sinks into me, the more the red and white colors merge together. And right over my belly, where his head rests, together we are a fiery fuchsia sunset.

I stare into the blaze of us melting and mingling, my brain lucid and fluid.

"Remember when we first got here," Roman says, sleepily, his words dancing like playful fireflies before me, "when Phoenix left us alone … when she went to go talk to Ansel?"

"Mm hmm." My affirmation comes from deep inside as I gently stroke my fingers through his thick hair.

"And remember when you were just about to kiss me …" He reaches over and wraps his arm around my leg, his skin so warm against mine.

"Yeah," I say, transfixed by the blazing sunset that rises off my stomach now and extends down my leg.

"Well … I was going to stop you," he says with the

tiniest hint of a smile in his voice.

"Oh, you were, huh?" I tease, wondering how he would've managed to do that, already hopelessly in love with me as he was.

"I was going to try, anyway."

"Do you think you would have succeeded?" I whisper, overcome by him.

"Probably not," he admits. "But maybe."

"Why were you going to stop me? Didn't you want to kiss me? If you already loved me …"

Now I was simply asking to hear it again, how much he loved me, even then. I don't think I'll ever tire of hearing Roman say that he's been secretly head over heels in love with me all along.

"More than anything," he says, flipping over, his elbows outside each of mine, his body pressed against me.

"I wanted to kiss you," he says, his eyes on me, then places a soft tiny kiss on my breast. "More than anything," he whispers, kissing me again, this time closing his eyes and moving up to my neck, "you could ever," he says slowly, gently kissing my collarbone, "imagine," he says, with the lightest, most delicate kiss yet, a kiss just under my earlobe that sends a surge of desire coursing through me, so deeply my toes curl and the sheets bunch in my hands.

"So what was the problem," I breathe, reaching up to

grasp his broad muscular shoulders, feeling them flex as he holds himself above me.

"I knew you didn't know me," he whispers, "not yet." He places tiny kisses all around my ear. I close my eyes, wanting to feel his breath and his words even more deeply, on more levels. There seems to be no end to how deep these sensations can travel into me.

"You *thought* you knew me, and yes I loved you, but you didn't know who I really was," he goes on whispering and kissing, "and I thought it wouldn't be right to let you kiss me, since I loved you so deeply, but to you, I was still only a crush."

"You thought I had a crush on you?" I ask, my eyes closed, smiling.

"No." He stops. "I *know* you had a crush on me," he clarifies, and I open my eyes to see him smiling, smoldering with confidence.

"Was it that obvious?" I ask.

"Honestly?"

"Of course, honestly! No, lie to me," I joke. But his face turns suddenly serious.

"If I could do one thing in the whole world, I would go back in time, and I would bottle, somehow, the look in your eyes whenever you saw me," he says, his voice as raw as his feelings. "It melted my heart, your big puppy dog eyes, because remember, I already knew about all our lives together, all our marriages, our ups and downs. And crushes, when they come, are like some kind of magical breeze from another dimension, and then they eventually fade; they always do. They give way to deeper love, sometimes. But getting to watch that gleam in your eyes, that hope in your soul, over me again, how your whole body lifted every time you saw me ..." He shakes his head in a kind of disbelief. "Why on earth do you think I found a way to run into you every single day?"

"So you could see it," I whisper, mesmerized by his words, memorizing every detail of the expression on his face in this moment and wondering what on Earth I ever did to deserve this rare and exquisite experience of love.

"So I could see it," he confirms, lingering just inches from my face, then moving in for a long passionate kiss while pressing the weight of his body into mine. The taste of him brings me to a place I've never known in this life, a wild untamed paradise. I wrap my arms around his neck and lose myself in it.

As the kiss begins to escalate into more, he stops to look at me. Both of us breathy and serious, then smiling at how helplessly we're overcome by each other.

"So let me get this straight," I say with a smirk. "You were going to *try* to stop me from kissing you because you thought it wouldn't be right for me?" I ask. Grabbing his warm scruffy face in my hands, not caring about the words so much as wanting to keep melting into his eyes as he talks.

He thinks about this. "I thought it wouldn't be right *of me*, on behalf *of you*."

I laugh, shaking my head, "You are my reward for something," I marvel, stroking his hair. And I don't say a word after that; neither of us does. I just pull him to me. We rest there in our tangled embrace. We just lie together, holding on to each other as hard as we can for the small amount of time we have left until we have to get up.

All around me is ice and snow. I stand alone, lost in a frozen landscape.

Looking down at my bare hands, I realize they should be frostbitten—but they're not even cold.

I watch the Arctic winds blast across the frozen tundra, whipping snow into vortexes, not feeling even the slightest chill, knowing I should be hypothermic or even long dead from exposure—

That's one of the things telling me this is a dream.

Cian's voice calling out from some distance behind me is the other.

"Eve," he says, sounding like he always does, no hurry at all in his relaxed tone, my name traveling easily through the howling winds. I close my eyes for a brief second, just taking in his voice. I don't answer him. I don't even turn around. When I open my eyes again, I just keep staring off into the harsh frozen wilderness sprawling out before me.

Alaska.

The northernmost tip of the continent. The place Jude is from, which he described to me, in elaborate detail, mere minutes after we first met.

It's now the setting of my latest reoccurring dream. It's an ominous one, and it always starts out the same. I stand alone, quietly marveling at the wildly dangerous beauty, knowing I should be cold, realizing I'm not, hearing Cian's voice behind me without answering him or turning around.

And there's always a caribou perched high on a distant ridge. He's colossal, and he seems to stare at me. He *is* staring at me. A plume of white frost from his mighty breath materializes in sync with my heartbeats. His incredible span of antlers turn in my direction, his gaze steady and unwavering. There's something he's trying to tell me.

"Eve," Cian says again, sounding noticeably closer, his voice a bit sharper too.

But I don't turn around. The sun is coming up now, and I'm watching the long blue shadows it casts on the snow, the shapes of spruce trees shifting into other things.

There's a heavy base of thick powder packed in below the caribou's ridge, and I'm transfixed by the dashes of brilliant yellow light that suddenly makes it shine. Sunlight spilling like paint between the massive evergreens, splashing a wave of golden warmth onto the frozen jade lake that stretches from the periphery of the woods, far in the distance, all the way to the tips of my toes at its opposite edge.

I hear the crunch of snow behind me—Cian's footsteps.

"I'm right here, Eve," he says, more emphatic now, more urgent, his voice just behind my head. He places his hand on my shoulder, like he's trying to give me some proof of his presence.

But instead of turning around and looking at him, instead of taking the chance to see my grandfather's face again, I stare at the sparkling crystals of ice as the rising sun lights them up, like a billion loose diamonds scattered across the vast sheet of solid mineral green before me.

"I know," I halfheartedly tell him, but somehow I don't know—even as I feel his hand on my shoulder and hear his voice just behind me. In my heart, I doubt somehow that he's really there.

Still yet to turn and look at him, my eyes are focused on a particular spot, on one crystal of ice, one shining diamond, which appears to be perched a millimeter higher than the rest.

I start walking toward the spot, overcome with the sudden strong feeling that Cian is actually *there* and not behind me.

"I have to go, okay?" I call back toward the snowy bank, my eyes focused forward on where I think he is, and take a few steps onto the sheer green pane of ice. Mentally, I'm still waiting for his reply from behind me. The farther I walk, the more slippery it becomes and the more not hearing a response from Cian begins to bother me. I raise my arms out from my sides, trying to keep my balance. But my feet go out from under me and I crash to the ice.

I begin hearing tiny snaps, like brittle bones fracturing beneath me. But the steadily increasing noise of ice splintering isn't what unnerves me.

It's not hearing Cian reply.

"Cian?" I call to him, shrill, still facing away from the shoreline from my prone position on the ice.

As I slowly get to my feet, I contemplate stealing a glance back behind me for the first time. If only I can drag my eyes off the spot they're focused on, but the idea fills me with dread. Something bad will happen if I look away.

"Cian!" I shout, but my throat-burning scream is weak, muffled by the howling wind, and only answered by more silence.

The anxiety growing too much to bear, I drag my eyes up

from the ice. The first thing I see is that the caribou has vanished from the ridge. Then I notice that huge swaths of snow are gone too, and what little is left is rapidly melting before my eyes, like in a time-lapse photograph. It's almost instantly replaced by patches of churned-up earth and thick pools of mud as an increasingly large river of snowmelt runs off down the rocks toward where I'm standing near the center of the frozen lake.

With the sense that doom is impending, I give a quick half-turn, heart full of dread, glancing behind me at the shore. I look all around, but I don't see my grandfather anywhere.

He was never behind me, I realize, just as I'd thought all along.

Then what were snaps and splinters a second ago turn to thunderous cracks and fractures. Hands over my ears trying to muffle the incredible noise threatening to split my brain down the middle, I whip back around just in time to see a raging flood descending from the mountains and a fissure opening up from the tip of my front toe and splitting the ice like a napkin torn in two. Both forces are in a race toward one another, toward the very spot where I'd been focusing—

Where Cian's nightstand now rests.

The thought of watching Cian's nightstand fall through

the ice is an unspeakable horror that screams in my head. My feet to break into a sprint, away from the safety of the shore, toward the peril of the unknown, or perhaps the absolute certainty of a painful death.

In a race with the splitting ice, I dash for the nightstand. It's all I have left of my grandfather—somehow it *is* my grandfather. Just as I get close enough to grasp at it, the ice rips apart, and the frigid water consumes the nightstand like doll furniture, in a single monstrous gulp.

Without hesitation, I dive in after it, but it sinks quickly, as if it's already completely filled with water—*or something else, something even heavier*. I swim downward as fast as I can, but it's falling away from me twice as fast, careening down into an endless abyss of ever-increasing darkness.

My final view of it is of the familiar ornate carving on the front. I stare helplessly as it rushes away from me. Squinting my eyes, I see the Animus symbol light up, glowing cobalt blue, almost pulsing within the larger design. The carving, it appears, always contained the Animus symbol. It was hidden in plain sight all along.

What is Cian trying to tell me about Animus? What did he know?

As the last sight of the glowing symbol is swallowed up, my lungs ignite, burning with the mind-numbing fire of total oxygen deprivation.

Frantic, I look toward the surface, but I've drifted to where there's only solid ice above me. I move along the ice desperately, searching for an opening, pounding on what looks like two feet of solid frozen water.

That's when Jude's face appears. He's looking down at me through the ice. His polar blue eyes, mirrors of the Arctic winter sky behind him, are bolted to mine. I notice right away that he isn't panicked. Not in the least. He's not trying to rescue me either. He just watches me, almost curiously, not understanding why I would pound against an impenetrable barrier, like a savage wild animal no less.

"You don't have to do that," he informs me, brows furrowed, his angelic face truly bewildered. And even though he whispers from the other side of the ice, his voice echoes like a loud speaker through the water all around me.

Don't have to do what? Get stuck under here? Jump into the water? Walk out onto the ice in the first place? *What?* I think but can't manage to say.

"Whenever you're ready," he tells me.

Then his eyes soften. His mouth rises into a serene little smile as a pulse of what can only be described as pure love emanates from him, consuming me.

I feel completely safe.

He repeats the words he spoke to me on the cliff in Rugby, but this time he doesn't speak out loud. I hear his voice, his words, as he thinks them into my mind:

You can't lose your life because you don't have a life. You are life.

I'm ready, I tell him without hesitation, in the same wordless way, and a wave of relief washes over me, and everything inside quits struggling.

I feel myself relax, melting into the water. I become part of it as I drift back from the ice, away from the surface, knowing I'm not going to live and feeling nothing but incredible peace. I allow myself to float downward into the abyss, my eyes staying locked on his as more and more space grows between us. Though I feel my lungs fill with water, it doesn't bother me.

I'm drifting away from him, but something inside tells me that I'm drifting closer. I know I'm getting closer.

At the last second he raises his hand, as if to wave goodbye, but more like he's waving hello, and I see something shining on his palm—a symbol, the letter M glowing golden in the natural lines of his hand.

Out of some instinct, I look down, holding out my own hand. As it floats weightlessly before me in the water I see the same brilliant shimmering M spanning my right palm … And the abyss closes in and everything around me goes black.

I sit up, choking and gasping for air, my eyes darting around the dark room.

The same way I have woken up for as long as I can remember, with the same dream, only this time it lingers in my mind—Cian, the water, the nightstand, and Jude's face, all beating like a pulse in my brain.

When my breathing begins to slow, I reach for Roman, feeling the sheets next to me. He isn't there. I look toward the bathroom, but it's dark. No sign that he's in there either.

So I jump up and race to the light switch on the wall, heart beating out of my chest, fearing he's not here. Then seeing.

Roman is gone—along with any sign he was ever here.

NINE

— ✠ —

A large screen descends out of the ceiling.

After watching it for a moment, still in shock as it makes its smooth trip down into place, I think to grab a sheet off my bed and wrap it around myself just before Jakob's face flicks onto the screen.

"Eve, good morning," he says, looking straight ahead instead of directly at me. It has the feeling of a prerecording. "I know you're just beginning to find your way around our beloved ancient enclave and that you've still got so much to learn and discover about the way we do things here. One of the first things you'll need to know is that *this* is how we communicate. These retractable monitors are virtually everywhere. Antiquus is a very big place, as I'm sure you've noticed, so we use a lot of technology to help us all stay in touch.

"There are two other pieces of equipment on the table by your door—your wireless headphones and your tablet. They're both incredibly user friendly and incredibly important, so you'll want to have them on you at all times. They'll help you find your way to Cian's service this morning —the location is already programmed in—and with everything else you'll ever need to know around here." He smiles. "See you soon."

Jakob's face and voice cut out, replaced by the seal of Antiquus and soothing music. The time, 5:25 A.M., blinks in the corner of the screen—I had no idea how late it is. Maybe Roman just went to his own room to get ready and decided to let me sleep. I hurry to the bathroom, but Sourial's familiar voice stops me in my tracks.

"This is your morning news update. Unrest overnight in Primitus; officials are not sure what led to the violent outbreak." Her concerned face is replaced by images of raging fires in a walled desert refuge. "Residents in the Warrior sector claim to have been peacefully protesting over scarce resources, but leaders are claiming that a small group of agitators were rioting and looting. The citizens of Primitus are still expected to vote on the ratification of Aurora as scheduled.

"Meanwhile, Antiquus and Primitus outposts are now operational on the continents of Australia and Europe.

Animus testing continues across the region and across the globe. All unordered soul assimilation is expected to end worldwide in less than a week, as the complete halt of apocalyptic events continues."

The screen flicks off and glides back up into the ceiling.

My thoughts are on the violence in Primitus and on Jude as I near the entrance to the Subterranean, a ten-foot-tall steel door, like a bank vault for a giant. The second I approach, it gently slides open, and a red light above the door begins to flash. First slowly, then with ever increasing speed until it's blinking so rapidly that I find myself hurrying inside. I stand at the beginning of a long steel walkway, an enclosed tube about eight feet around.

It takes me a few minutes to get to the other end, but as I do, I start to hear a melodic chanting. Not words, but musical notes made with human voices, rising all around me. The hair on my arms stands on end as I enter the inside of a massive mountain that's been completely hollowed out. The Subterranean stretches thousands of feet overhead and thousands of feet in every direction. What looks like a million candlelit caves are carved out, covering every wall around the large circular dome and as far up as I can see. Prayer and meditation and white robes are everywhere I look.

As I clutch Cian's urn in my hands, the tiny clicks coming from the heels of the ballet flats on my feet make me feel as small as an ant as I walk through the vast cavern. The people here seem to float instead of walk through the uncluttered expanse, and even at six-thirty in the morning, the living space of the Mountain souls is humming.

Jakob comes striding up, seeming too overly excited to see me given the occasion that brings us here.

"You look beautiful," he says, pulling me in for a hug that I want no part of. I wait till he's done comforting me like a limp fish, trying not to asphyxiate in his overpowering cologne.

"Is Roman here?" I ask when he finally lets me go.

"Eve," he says with almost an annoyed look, "Roman was given free rein to care for you, whatever he needed to do and wherever he needed to go to do that. That was his job for six long weeks. All of it was carefully monitored, meticulously documented. You were very ill." He squints his eyes like he's trying to understand exactly what I experienced, as if he was observing me the entire time. "But since that's no longer the case," he smiles at me, "now Roman has to follow the same rules as everyone else."

"What rules are those?"

"For starters, he stays with his own collective during the day—*and* at night." He raises his eyebrows at me with more than a hint of disapproval. I wonder exactly how much he knows—if *that* was being monitored as well. And a chill rushes down my spine at the thought of Jakob, or anyone else, watching me with Roman.

"You see Roman has another job to do now because *everyone* has a job to do here. That provides us a certain order. Order is *everything*, and it is everywhere—a divine order, actually; you can see it in our ancient network of castles, surrounded by what look like chaotic labyrinths of gardens but are actually elaborately interconnected and meticulously organized. And all of this miraculously mimicking the constellation Orion in the night sky above."

ORION

My knees wobble with a sudden slight weakness at his last few words. "What did you say?"

"This entire place is built to be a reflection of Orion," he repeats, and in a split second I go someplace. As I stand there listening to him, I travel inside my own brain with the whole of my entire consciousness, while also keeping perfect eye contact with Jakob and listening to his every word.

I descend into a maze of darkness, winding around fleshy gray matter, sifting through lobes and cortexes. I'm on a search, past flashes of neurons and synapses firing like lightning bolts from one spot to another, until I come to what I'm looking for—lateral ventricles, elongated ridges, my hippocampus, where I've stored a certain very early childhood memory.

I watch my own hand reach out and touch this ridged area of my brain. With an instant bright flash, I'm careening at the speed of light. All around me is brilliant bright purple and red—interstellar clouds of dust and gas, nebula surrounded on all sides by blackness, the total dark of deep space.

Then I arrive. Suddenly, I'm standing in front of calm blue waters.

It's the central Macedonian region of northern Greece, a town on a peninsula called Halkidiki. I breathe in salty air, enchanted by the smell of olive and lemon trees and by the fig in my hand, round and dark purple with a tiny green stem. I bite into the skin of the soft, sun-warmed fruit, which breaks easily, and the seedy flesh dissolves into my mouth with the sweetness of honey and the taste of bright apple and smooth pear.

"It is the birthplace of Aristotle," I hear Cian remark of the beautiful coastal paradise. Then he and I are climbing a handful of white stone steps into the town's small library. The space is filled with dusty old books on dusty old shelves. A squat dark-haired Greek woman named Naida shows us to a back room, which is even older and dustier, where she believes rests a certain text that Cian has been searching for.

I sit in a hard wooden chair at a large table made of pine. Volumes of ancient books lay open all across the room, covering the floor, the table, the chairs—every possible surface. Rulers, protractors, and pencils scattered about as a much younger Cian mills around the small space like a bumbling mad scientist, one who's just realizing he's beginning to put together the first few ingredients of the atom bomb.

Outside the small square window beside me, Shamus is fishing. Tall and skinny, twenty-five years old, standing on rocks in cut-off jeans at the water's edge of the Aegean Sea, casting a line from a long wooden pole into the water. I'm seven and a half years old and wearing my hair in braids, as I always did then, and the white eyelet dress I loved so much, watching Shamus cast his line into the crystal blue sea—and apparently also listening very carefully as Cian talks to himself.

"The sign opposite in the sky from Ophiuchus is Orion," he says as he pages through a big ancient book. "Ophiuchus sits in the general direction toward the center of our galaxy, which the ancients called 'The Gate of the Gods.'"Orion sits in the opposite direction, which would be considered the anti-galactic center; the ancients called this direction "The Gate of Man." He stops and ponders, tapping a pencil against his temple.

Then I snap back to Jakob and his rambling monologue.

"Again, Eve, this was all part of *their* plan for us and for our survival. They were connected." He points up to the heavens. "The Three, as we call them. Connected in ways we're only just beginning to understand. And according to them, people must be organized too. Grouped into categories by their soul age and housed accordingly: a perfect arrangement of humanity for optimal promise, productivity, and social order."

"The newest of the Old Souls are the Sages, where Roman is being ... *accommodated*," he emphasizes, a clear threat, an unsubtle flex of his power. "With INs from 300 to 499, these are the thinkers, philosophers, artists, poets, and gurus. They invent, they innovate, they keep us progressing, and they also provide guidance, like Orias, who I often seek for council. Living in a part of Antiquus referred to as the Towers, they're nestled like birds in the endless peaks and spires that ascend into the sky, where they can keep their heads where they belong, comfortably in the clouds."

He smiles in a mocking way. "The next oldest are the Dragons, with INs over 500. These are the leaders of Antiquus, the political types, the tycoons—if there was an economy, which there is not—not yet. The Dragons handle daily operations, logistics, running the Animus Task Force, and some very light decision-making. They live in the Foundation—it's the main floor, sprawling through the whole of Antiquus.

"The Mountain souls, since they are older than the Dragons, live lower—that's how this works, the older the soul, the lower they live. The Mountains have lived one thousand lifetimes or more. They pray and meditate on a rigorous schedule, and they're also the keepers of our environment. And, as you can see, they live in this mysterious place, the Subterranean. The official name for where *you* live, by the way, which is nearly a half-mile beneath the surface, accessible only through your private labyrinth of tunnels, is called the Catacomb." He says this last bit without much expression.

I swallow at the name Catacomb—an underground burial chamber—and start to fear the real reason why I'm alone down there.

"You didn't mention when a person goes from being a Mountain soul to being a Zodiac soul," I say. "What's the IN for when someone becomes a Zodiac?"

"There isn't one," he says, dusting off the front of his pants. "Bit of housekeeping. Your grandfather's ashes will be kept here on display within the sacred temple. May I?"

I hand over Cian's urn, surrendering all I have left of him, and answering Jakob's question just the way he wants, with my silent obedience.

"Shall we?" he asks, and again I do as he wishes, following him toward the temple.

We walk through one of the small candlelit caves, which looks a lot like all the other small candlelit caves. Only we keep walking farther and farther into it. As we do, the walls gradually become wider and the ceiling higher until we arrive at the back of it, which is a space as large as any church. It's wafting with incense and brimming with candles and flowers. At the front, an altar clothed in white and a pulpit, and between there and where we stand are rows and rows of wooden folding chairs all filled with people robed in white.

"Did they know my grandfather?" I ask.

"Yes. He spent a lot of time in Antiquus before he passed. He was here waiting for people to start arriving. He was the first person every Mountain soul met. He didn't hide away," Jakob whispers, "like some of the others. He insisted on being with the people. And they loved him very much, as you can see."

"Wow," I say, overwhelmed by the staggering number of people whose lives my grandfather touched.

"And I always felt our life was so small," I marvel to myself out loud, giving Jakob the impression I'm confiding in him.

"Did you?" he asks, like the uninteresting details of my previously quiet and boring life fascinate him. "Well, you may have thought that, but it was never true. Small is not in your destiny."

I look around the room, at what must be two or three thousand people. I'm dazed by it, moved and proud of my grandfather's legacy.

"Look at them all," Jakob whispers into my ear. "And they adore you."

"They don't even know me."

"No, but they *feel* as if they do," he says, like it's exactly the same thing.

Jakob eulogizing Cian makes me want to vomit.

Not for any one specific reason, just a general bouquet of nauseous spastic reflexes at his every word and movement, a seasickness wafting through me as I sit in the front row, next to people I've never seen before, all of them smiling adoringly at me—the whole experience remarkably uncomfortable.

"When I tell you that Cian O'Cleirigh was an important man, I know my words are a failure. You see, mere words cannot convey the gravity of his contribution to us," he remarks, correctly.

I stare at Cian's ashes—twenty feet up, in the center of the high limestone wall, tucked into a large carved-out niche and surrounded by candles and flowers.

"Cian Malachi O'Cleirigh could wake the dead," he proclaims, to the audible shock of everyone in the temple and to my surprise as well. "Now I know this comes as somewhat astonishing news, as he himself never told any of you this, but his beautiful granddaughter, Evelyn, can attest to it." He motions in my direction, all eyes fall on me, and I give a small nod, *of course*, just as Jakob wants.

"He was able to wake the dead. The waker, as those like him have been known throughout history. And he was here on a divine mission."

Jakob falls silent, seeming to disappear into his own mind. When he emerges his tone is vulnerable, like he just decided to share something that a big part of him thinks maybe he shouldn't—to me it looks like nothing more than a stellar acting performance.

"It was a car accident—a two-lane rural highway," he says, his voice low and weak. "There was this sort of hissing sound when I came to, and I felt warm. Not like sitting under a blanket on a cold night warm, no. This was pure radiance, the most glowing, radiant warmth emanating from me and onto me all at once. It seemed to envelop me inside and out. It seemed to *be* me, somehow—it was life I was feeling, which really is love."

I watch those near me nod their heads in knowing.

After taking a few heavy breaths, he reaches for the nearby bottle of water and downs several large gulps, which can be heard through the microphone. Even if he is acting, which I'm beginning to second-guess, I could never imagine Jakob acting as human as he seems in this moment, as vulnerable as the rest of us. His usual "relatable yet simultaneously larger-than-life" persona has been completely stripped away. And the silence gripping the thousands of people gathered tells me that everyone is feeling the same thing.

Shamus was always there, each and every time Cian brought the dead back to life, but I was only present for a small handful. I don't really know if this claim that Jakob is teeing up is true.

"The hissing noise was coming from the overturned tractor trailer ... from the smoldering undercarriage. I only took my eyes of the road for a second." Jakob pauses again, looking lost in thought. Or guilty.

"There were others involved. There was the driver of the truck, of course. He was killed instantly, and there were passengers with me as well, but—"

Again he breaks off. Presumably he's about to say that Cian only woke him. I begin to visualize the scene he's describing. That's when it hits me like a punch in the gut. The two-lane rural highway, the overturned tractor trailer, hissing, driver killed instantly, others, all dead, his eyes, his voice—

He is Thomas Greeley.

Cian woke *him*, Thomas Greely, and I was there to see it. The disturbed young man in his twenties, his stunned face and shaking body both soaked red, who I witnessed rise from death in the middle of the blood-stained asphalt on that bizarre night in Sulphur, Nevada. The young man, who we drove fifty miles to a gas station, looked very different from the put-together and controlled leader of Antiquus before me now—the person who, apparently, is too critical to the history or survival of humanity to die there in the desert.

But still, how on Earth have I not noticed? *How have I not remembered him?* I wonder, questioning the lucidness of my own mind.

Wondering if this wasn't all some dream, I stare at Cian's urn, surrounded by orange and purple and crimson flowers of every variety. And as I watch, the bright flowers morph into a pile of white lilies. I look around to see if anyone else is seeing what I'm seeing. When I look back, the flowers have turned colorful again.

"The loss of Cian O'Cleirigh means many things. It's the end of one world and the beginning of a new one, a world where order is now our guiding light. We note this, of course, with the commencing of Year Zero, on the day after Cian's death, recognizing that we have crossed over from one era to another. The world in which the fate of humanity could be aided, kept on course, that world ended with Cian's passing. The Sages have all confirmed that he was to be the last. That humanity must forge ahead now without any means of course correction. That is why we must rely *completely* on order in this new world.

"Our only comfort is that he went peacefully. That much we know. And so we thank this great man for his critical contributions to the human race, and we ask that from beyond this world he continue to defend the light, just as he once did for all of us. Continue to awaken truth and justice and righteousness in humankind."

People begin to leave the space after waiting in line to pay their respects by walking past his urn high above their heads. Jakob stands near the altar, talking with a few white robed men. I stand in the back, where I've been told to wait.

I am waiting like the good little drone I feel myself becoming, a choiceless, opinionless, person-bot who sleeps alone, under surveillance, in a pre-dug grave that can be filled in at any time. And of all the millions of things I have to wonder about—where Roman is, the connection between Ophiuchus and Orion, the role of the Aion Dorea in Aurora and Animus, the fall of Egypt, my disturbing dream, the letter M, Cian's will, Jakob being Thomas Greely—I'm not wondering a single thing. I'm just standing there. Wondering feels like too big of a liability.

"Don't you just hate that guy," someone says, exactly what I'd be thinking as I watch Jakob, if I were allowing myself to think.

I turn to see a man standing beside me, also facing the altar, his hands clasped behind his back. It's the same man who brushed against me on the way to conclave, the one in the green cape with the salt and pepper hair and glasses. Though now he's in a white robe.

"Why?" I ask him in a low voice, remembering his strange secretive smile, deciding to risk it. "Is it because he somehow managed to make Cian's funeral all about himself?"

"In the most convincingly genuine way?" he asks, his mouth barely moving, his words dying to silence just past my ear.

"Is it that," I ask, "or the subtle propagandizing?" I look at Jakob, who's still deep in conversation but glancing over at me every third second or so.

"Oh, you mean the way he speaks for everyone? Expressing—brilliantly, no less—what everyone is feeling and then sliding in something he'd like to add to the narrative?"

"Like the fact that since Cian woke him he represents truth and justice and righteousness? It might interest people to know that he woke Shamus as well."

"When Shamus had that accident, and he hit the tree," the man says.

"How on Earth do you know about that?" I ask the stranger, breathless. I turn to steal a glance, but he's gone. I look back, and Jakob's eyes are on me. The second he turns back to the person he's talking to, I slip out and start running as fast as I can.

PART TWO

MERCURY

TEN

Nothing I've learned about Antiquus over the past twenty-four hours could have prepared me for who Rafe is, or for seeing the Towers.

The second I reach the mouth of the cave that opens up into the expanse of the Subterranean, I hear him whisper my name.

"Eve." His back is against the wall right next to the opening of the cave. "Hand me your headphones and tablet."

I hand them over, noting a strange lost feeling as I do—a fear of being disconnected. How will I know where I am going? Do I really trust this guy?

Another white-robed man walks by, takes my electronics from him, and just keeps walking without a word.

"Come on," the first man says to me, and I follow him

in the direction of the exit.

"Who are you?" I whisper as we stride quickly but calmly through the massive space.

"Rafe."

"Okay, *Rafe*, but that's just a name. Who are you, really?"

I find out that and a lot more when we arrive at the Towers, the mind-bending home of the Sage collective. Twenty-six mammoth spires are staggered out in what appears to be a strange, random arrangement over the entire complex of Antiquus.

But as Rafe explains, "Their placement actually aligns to the polygon pattern of the Orion constellation." He goes on to tell me that each colossal luminescent gothic tower is interconnected—tubes of metallic glass, stronger than steel and all but invisible, span from one spire to the next.

"So Sages from one discipline can 'collaborate'," he air-quotes, "with Sages from another. Each tower houses Sages according to whatever they excel at—music, literature, art, astronomy, technology, science, theology, mysticism, quantum and meta-physics, and so on."

As I follow Rafe up the long circular staircase, I peer out a small window and see green robes floating through the sky as Sages walk from one spire to the next.

"Almost a thousand feet off the ground," he remarks, "like phantoms on a mission."

We arrive at the technology tower, an enormous circular open space buzzing with green-robed people. They appear to be deep into the research and development of some kind of headwear gadget.

"Oculum, a dream come true," Rafe remarks. "The next generation virtual reality headsets. Miraculous. Craft the message, control the flow of information, and beam it directly into my head." He leers at a Sage working nearby, heavy on the sarcasm, but the tall man just stares at Rafe.

"Splendid! Why not?" Rafe asks, picking one up. "Better yet, make it an augmented reality game." Sages are blindly walking around testing the headsets, swiping at the air, bumping into desks and into one another. "Tell them who to love, who to hate, what to think, what *not* to think. Spy on your human drones with ease, all through the most addicting game ever created," He sounds like he's making an ironic commercial for the device, "with Oculus." He haphazardly tosses it back on the table.

"How do you know about my brother?" I ask. "About his accident?"

"Eve, I lived on your street … *in Rugby*. We were practically neighbors." He sounds amazed I don't know that. And then I remember.

"The house across the street, the green one," I say, as I picture him watering his lawn in red swim trunks, an unlit cigar hanging from his lips.

"And I thought *I* lived in my own world," he remarks with the hint of a smile.

"Sorry, I was sort of like an island unto myself," I say, feeling a tug for how simple my life used to be. "But that was then. So, exactly how much trouble am I going to be in for coming up here?"

"None," he says, matter-of-factly.

"Are you kidding? Jakob just told me all about how each person has to stay with their collective."

"Oh, which reminds me." He pulls the white robe over his head, revealing a green one underneath. Then he beckons me toward a large space filled with endless arrays of monitors and hulking servers.

"Welcome to hacker heaven," he smiles, then hangs the white robe on a rack, right next to a black one. "To answer your question, there are *not* a lot of rules here, very few actually—official ones anyway. But there are a great deal of *unwritten* rules."

"Enforced by the power of suggestion," I speculate.

"And fear of the unknown," he adds.

"And the flawlessly crafted illusion of free will."

"Bingo." He points at me as we arrive at the computers.

"You win the game. Congratulations, your prize is paranoia," he announces.

"Sometimes paranoia's just having all the facts," a monotone voice pipes up.

"Collins," Rafe says. "Thinks he was some great beatnik novelist in his last life."

"William Burroughs died in '97; I was born in '98. What more proof do you need?" Collins asks from somewhere, still out of sight.

Rafe rolls his eyes. "So ... Eve, to answer your earlier question. Yes, you're correct, everyone *does* have to stay within his or her own collective. Much easier to keep us bickering amongst ourselves when we're neatly separated by the identities they've created and constantly reinforce."

He slides into a seat surrounded by twenty computer screens, all facing him like sunflowers. "Yes, everyone must stay with the souls of his or her designated collective at all times ... everyone, that is, except for you." The screens all light up at once with a single swipe of his hand. He reaches for the unlit cigar resting on one of the keyboards and pops it into his mouth.

"What?" I ask.

"Oh, did Jakob not mention that?" he asks, not really asking, as he types. "The only chess piece in the whole game that can move freely about the board."

"The queen …" I say, not entirely sure what he means by that.

Rafe snaps his fingers, points in my direction, then returns to banging away on his keyboards.

Collins chuckles from his hidden space nearby.

"I'm sorry; I just can't get enough of it. It's legendary."

I walk around Rafe's desk and see my face on at least ten screens in a three-second video clip, a close-up of the moment I leaned in toward Jakob and whispered "the illusion of choice" and then the stunned look on his face.

It plays over and over again on a loop.

"Collins, honestly, how many times are you going to watch that?" Rafe asks.

"Is everything being monitored?" I ask Collins. He's watching not only the footage of my exchange with Jakob, but also every other imaginable thing going on in and around Antiquus. People's bathrooms, showers, beds, boring stuff, people working, one guy picking his nose, some static surveillance videos, but most from handheld cameras—the tablets people are holding to their own faces or have set next to them.

"You can see everywhere?" I ask. "*Everything?*"

Collins looks up at me. He has a gaunt frame, a baby face, a mess of spiky blond hair, and serious bags under his eyes, "Yeah," he says, his voice gentle, a conciliatory look on his thin face. "I've been deleting stuff for you," he says with a little proud smile. "Here and there, when I can."

"You have? Thank you," I say. He smiles, blushes a little.

"I'm like a ghost in the mainframe," he brags, shyly, pointing to another screen, one filled with scrolling lines of code.

"You read code," he guesses after I look at the screen for a bit too long.

"Eh, a little."

"I should warn you," Rafe says. "Collins is madly in love with you, as you've probably figured out by now. If he had any idea what you could do with a computer, you'd be in serious trouble."

"*He's* the one who's in love with you," Collins whispers. "So ... what *can* you do with a computer?"

"Eve." It's Roman's voice. I look up to see him striding toward me with another young Sage.

"I'm so sorry," he says as he pulls me into a warm hug. "They made me leave. And then I couldn't ..." He looks down, upset about missing Cian's funeral.

"I know. Trust me, I understand," I say, trying to ease his mind. "Who's your friend?"

"I'm Seth." He's tall and thin with a military-style buzz cut and the same dark circles under his eyes as Collins. "It's good to finally meet you ... in person anyway." He shakes my hand then takes a seat at a nearby terminal.

"We just met," Roman says of Seth.

"Yeah, I just met Rafe," I say. Rafe waves at Roman, "And Collins." Collins leans out to look at Roman.

"Hey," Roman says with a small wave, but Collins just stares at him for a second then retracts his head behind his wall of monitors.

Roman gives me a look like *What's with him?*

"Apparently I have an admirer," I whisper.

He smiles. "Smart guy."

"Have you never been in here before?" I ask, as Roman seems to be looking around as much as I am.

"No, I've hardly spent any time in the Towers at all. I was always with you. But now I'm getting a new job. Apparently I'm fit for engineering. That's about ten towers over from here."

"He's got good looks *and* the highest IQ of any Sage, so yeah, it's his first day, and we all already hate him," Seth says.

"The two of you can exchange hairstyling tips later," Rafe says. "Let's not waste time. We've got a lot to cover."

Roman and I walk toward Rafe's chair, where he's hard at work banging away on multiple keyboards as lines of code scroll continuously on the monitors surrounding him. "First things first, don't drink the water," he instructs us without looking up.

"What are we supposed to drink?" Roman asks.

"Anything else," Rafe says, dead serious. "I mean it; drink maple syrup, anything but the water." He cues up video footage of the aquifers running underneath the gardens. As the water rushes by, millions of roots dangle into it from above. "Devil's breath."

"Devil's breath? Do you mean scopolamine?" I ask, referring to a plant I saw the effects of once while in Colombia with Cian.

"What's that?" Roman asks.

"Let's just say it makes people highly suggestible," Seth says.

"Removes free will," Collins clarifies.

"It basically turns them into total zombies," Rafe says.

"Blackout zombies, if given in large quantities," I say. "And in more diluted doses ... voting zombies, I suppose." This must be why I've felt my own sense of will slipping in and out, why I didn't notice the Thomas Jakob connection, and why Roman hadn't pieced together things that I would have expected him to.

"Exactly," Rafe says. "You know those really beautiful flowers that for whatever reason no one seems to think is all right to pick?" The white Christmas roses that Roman didn't want me to touch, the ones now filling Rafe's computer screen. "A genetically enhanced hellebore plant, or

Christmas Rose, which you've been subtly led to believe will burn the skin. Crossed with scopolamine hydrobromide."

Then Rafe pulls up another screen, one with strange patterns and a long green barcode. It's a spectrogram.

"It's the anthem," I say, easily reading the visual representation of the sound frequencies.

"Damn," Collins whispers.

"Yup," Rafe says. "There are lots of messages embedded in this one, from the flowers burning your skin to the ultimate superiority of old souls over new."

"And here—" I point. "'Forget about where you came from.'"

Seth and Rafe share a look.

"What?" I ask.

"Look, this is *unconfirmed*, okay?" Rafe says. "To say the least, so take it with a grain of salt, but we think we've intercepted communications ... from places other than Antiquus and Primitus."

"From Rugby?"

"Among others."

"Do they know?" I ask, noting the people nearby, busily working away. "About the water, the anthem, about any of this…"

"We've told them," Seth says. "All of it, repeatedly."

"They don't believe us," Rafe adds.

"Rafe, Collins, and I are considered ... troublemakers, outliers, fringe dwellers," Seth says. "They don't associate with our kind."

"Sages range from the bumbling and brilliant to the high-strung and harebrained," Rafe says. "They are wunderkinds and wizards of all sorts, and we are the weirdoes of the weirdoes."

"So is that why you brought me here?" I ask. "Since I'm the ultimate outcast, are you inviting me to join your merry band of weirdoes?" I smile.

"Kind of," Rafe says. "We're here to help you, actually."

"Help me with what?"

Rafe, Seth, and Collins share a heavy look. Collins motions us all over to his workspace where he cues up a video. Valeria Porter's tear-soaked face fills the screen. She wipes her cheek with the back of her hand.

"Eve," she says, "if you get this video ..." Her face wrenches with emotional distress. "God, I hope you get this video." She takes a deep breath and pulls herself together. "I'm in Primitus because my IN is 122. I should be a Guardian soul, but I don't get to ... I'm being forced to stay with Shamus, where the King souls live."

Valeria breaks off, and I feel a sick turn in my stomach about what all of that may mean. "I got separated from Porter in all the chaos that happened right after you left

Rugby. I was brought here. I don't know where Porter is."

Once again, she has to stop to compose herself. "The baby's fine." She moves the camera down to show her belly, virtually unchanged. "Not growing now or progressing, it seems, but perfectly healthy, so I'm told … and I'm all right. There's a lot of chaos outside the King sector, and I'm afraid … for the baby … I'm afraid of what they'll do to me here. I'm afraid of your brother." She's openly crying now. "And all he keeps saying is that you're the only one who can help me." Then her eyes dart around as if she's heard a noise and the video goes black.

"When was this?" I ask.

"Two weeks ago," Rafe says.

Two weeks ago? I think of the violence I saw on the news just this morning, and my heart sinks.

"All right," I say, voice shaking. "How are you guys going to help me with this?"

"Well, first let's tell you what we think," Rafe says, his eyes on Seth.

"We think it's a trap," Seth says.

I nod. "That he's trying to draw me in. But why? If Shamus had wanted to kill me, he could have. He had every chance; there's some reason he didn't, something he needs from me. That's what I've been thinking, anyway."

"Yeah," Rafe says. He shares a look with Collins and Seth.

"What?" Roman asks.

"He needs your blood," Seth says. "He wants you alive, yes ..."

"*What?*" I ask.

"We'll tell you everything we know," Seth says, "but first, can you explain this to us?" He cues up more footage, this time of my room.

I'm alone in my bed, apparently sleeping, though my body shimmers and seems to flicker in and out of view like a hologram short-circuiting.

"What's happening to you?" Seth asks. "How are you doing this?"

"It happened a lot," Roman says.

Everyone is sort of huddling closer to hear what I have to say. I take a step toward the image, staring at it, watching how I pixelate in and out ... thinking of the places I was traveling to, a few of which I never want to think about again, much less discuss. Where do I even begin?

"We are ether," I start. "The body ... it's merely an energetic garment. Not unlike the robe you just peeled off," I say to Rafe. "It has many layers, or other bodies, within the vital body, one of which is an *astral* body."

The four of them study me like they might look at an alien describing another planet. "Anyone can do this," I say to the skeptical faces. "It's true. Roman, you did it the night you went to Eremis."

"No, *you* did it. I don't know how to ... project out of my body," he says. "One minute I was here in Antiquus, and the next minute we were someplace else."

"It's done with focus, harnessing this latent ability. The astral body is a vehicle. One that can be used to traverse ... all the starry regions, other dimensions, planes of existence, realms, things that are all around us all the time but hidden by the veil of a dense, unrealized, and unmanifested consciousness. You can take it places." I study the frozen image on the screen. "And it can take you places too; places you may not want to go."

"How do you know all this?" Seth asks.

"I just do," is all I say, not wanting to say how I know, that knowledge like this is just sent out everywhere, like free Wi-Fi, and that I'm not really sure why they can't see it. I don't think that's an answer they'll like to hear.

"*There* you are." Jakob's voice invades the space, and I jump at the sound of it as he comes striding toward us, his face pale, flanked by Karl Alastair and Marcus Joplin, the two Sage members of his High Commission, his *top advisers*, really just his eyes and ears in each collective.

"You know, you really shouldn't be spending time with that sort," Jakob says, presumably referring to Rafe,

Collins, and Seth, and likely Roman too. From the undeniably bratty quality of my silence, he knows that I'm now aware of what he conveniently neglected to tell me.

"Yes," he concedes, "you can go wherever you please, but Eve," he shakes his head, "there is so much good you can do here."

"Like manipulating people's minds—"

"Let me guess. We're poisoning the water supply and embedding hidden messages in the anthem." He snorts. "I really wish they'd come up with something more original—not a very creative bunch, unfortunately. And they're not playing with a full deck either, those three. Call them conspiracy theorists or whatever you want, but they've got an agenda of their own."

"What's that?" I ask.

"I don't know," he admits. "I really don't, but tell me this: why would we want to control people's minds when that is our single greatest resource?"

We walk into a lab where Sages in green lab coats work with high-powered microscopes and the most sophisticated scientific equipment I've ever seen. Jakob leads me over to a screen where he swipes through images as he talks, illustrating the realities of what he's telling me.

"Global starvation is inevitable, Eve," he says gravely, swiping through pictures of a scorched and barren landscape. "There are no crops … it's as if there are no bees at all." He sounds perplexed. "Some of our brightest Sages are working on artificial pollination but haven't mastered it yet, not even close. And there are no more fish in the sea; it seems something disrupted the food chain, and the predators went unchecked. And we're working on that too, on creating artificial habitats trying to repopulate salmon, bass, and other species that are rapidly becoming extinct, all from the stem cells we've managed to harvest. The land animals are dying as well; they'll all be dead in a season without any food. To say nothing of the lack of human conception worldwide."

He looks at me, his face studiously projecting dire alarm. "We must be extremely cautious, as a species, *reproductively*." He pauses here, his disapproval unmistakable, as if the nature of my relationship with Roman is some sort of an affront to the whole human race.

"You were saying," I drone, sounding unaffected by his attempt to shame me—and struggling not to feel ashamed.

"There are enormous problems in this world, Eve, dire problems. Yes, we're making progress in many ways, with Animus and the formation of Aurora, a single foundation for global peace, but—well, being who you are, with everything you know—Eve, my greatest hope is to work with you, side-by-side, me running Antiquus, and you presiding over all of it, leader of Aurora. Helping everyone in every collective. Teaching them, guiding them, as their one true leader. Tell me, why do you think you've been given such a private living space? Why do you think your seat in the great hall is front and center? Why do you think we've been so concerned about your health and your whereabouts?"

"You know what I think? I think you're full of shit... *Thomas*," I say, looking him square in the face. Returning my stare, he cocks his head. Eyes squinting.

"Eve, it was your own family who brought me into all of this in the first place. They knew who I was long before I did, *who I really am*. Your grandfather is the one who even suggested my name be changed in order to help me let go of the past, to embrace my future, and my destiny. He even chose Jakob," he reveals then studies me as my mind reels out of control. I'm struggling to understand it all, remembering Cian's hesitation to wake him, and Shamus' eagerness.

"And the Aion Dorea. Do you think they're are full of shit too?" he whispers, eyes darting around to be sure no one can hear us. "Because it was them who told me who you were, *who you really are*, why your IN is what it is. And what that really means." He pauses, seeming to debate whether or not to tell me.

"What?" I ask.

"That you are their queen," he whispers, seeming like he's taken aback even by the word itself, and I think of how Rafe just referred to me, the one queen on the chess board, the one who can go anywhere.

"They have been waiting for you. And *they* choose me so that I might protect you from people who are afraid of you. It appears our destinies are entwined. Because of my *unique* personality, they knew I would be able to convince people, like Karl Alastair, that you're not evil, that you're here to show the way, to enlighten us, to heal."

I'm reminded of the serpent bearer, but I remain unconvinced.

"People were afraid of you, weren't they?" he prods. "They were ..." He watches me begin to squirm. "Long before Animus came along ... you just wanted to be normal, didn't you?" he digs a bit more, watching how I grow uncomfortable. Insecure. Isolated all my life, a social outcast.

"People have always feared you. And do you know why?" he asks, and I feel like I'm about to get punched in the face. "It's because people are afraid of the truth, Eve," he says tenderly, echoing what Cian said to me so many times.

But I shake my head, not wanting to be convinced, not by him.

"Why don't I have a title? Huh?" he asks, his voice rising with frustration. "Tell me that. Because I am a placeholder, Eve. I've been preparing the way for you. *You* are the rightful leader of Aurora. You are the one. You'll have all the power. And you will get to appoint who you see fit to run Antiquus, and I hope it will be me."

His humble eyes are very convincing. "You know, those crazy Sages are right about one thing. There is a hidden truth here. And the truth is, we *don't* know how to fix this. We just don't. But we want people to feel safe and secure, so we tell them that everything's going to be fine. We lie. And there is no one other than you who is capable of cracking this code, of saving humankind from certain extinction. This is why your grandfather brought me back from the dead, so that I could prepare the way ... for you."

"Did he tell you that? Those exact words?" I ask, begging him with my eyes not to lie to me.

"Many times," he says, unwavering as steel.

He reaches into his pocket and pulls out a handwritten letter. One from Cian—dated the day before he died—and it backs up everything he's telling me.

ELEVEN

——— ✦ ———

I sleep with Roman that night.

Leaving my own room and walking all the way to his like I own the place. There is nothing I want more than to lie against his warm skin and have every part of him to myself, so that is what I am going to do. And when I finally make it all the way to the engineering tower, which is, quite possibly the farthest point from my isolated underground liar, and open the door to his bedroom, his eyes instantly light up.

"Now I want to bottle the look on *your* face," I say, closing the door behind me and crossing the long dorm room toward where he lie shirtless in his bed.

"Are you allowed to be in here?" he asks with alarm as I slip between the sheets and right up against him, no room to spare in his tiny twin bed.

"I can do whatever I want," I brag, running my hands under the blankets, across his warm hard stomach and up to his chiseled chest. Climbing on top of his body, lying the whole weight of myself on him, I rest my head on his chest, right up under his chin.

Roman takes a deep breath, inhaling the smell of me through the top of my head like a tranquilizer, and then slowly combs his fingers through my hair as we just lie there, holding on to each other. His touch sends chills from my ankles to my neck. He wraps his arms tight around me and squeezes, seeming scared to let go.

"What's bothering you?" I ask without looking up.

When he doesn't say anything, I start to worry a little.

"Is it Val, the video?" I am scared for her and have no idea what, if anything, I will be able to do about it. When Roman doesn't answer, I look up at him. He seems to be weighing whether or not to say what he is thinking.

"What is it?" I press.

"I hate him." His voice is dark and trembling slightly. "I mean that. I *hate* him." He lowers his tone to a whisper, as if someone can hear, reminding me that someone absolutely can. Jakob himself is very likely watching us right now.

Seeing as how I'm allowed to do whatever I want, I hop up and sashay across the room. I grab the roll of duct tape that

I'd spotted on the table when I came in, stretch out a long piece the full length of my arm, and rip it off with my teeth. I drag his desk chair over to where the retractable TV monitor comes down out of the ceiling. Even when it is retracted, it doesn't go completely flush with the ceiling, and the exposed inch and a half of the bottom is lined with microphones and cameras. I climb up onto the chair and cover the whole thing with the duct tape. Then I hop down and climb back into Roman's bed, scooting up against him on my side, wrapping my leg around his.

"I know you distrust him and see through him. I do too, but—"

"He wants you, Eve," Roman interrupts, staring at the ceiling. "He wants to *be* with you. He's infatuated with you, obsessed with you. And he wants to find a way to get rid of me. There, I said it. I've been feeling it since the second he knew he had to let me stay, that I was just a means to an end for him, a very temporary one."

It disturbs me to the core that Roman thinks Jakob wants me. Not just because I still feel some guilt about falling so hard for Jude so fast—guilt that is proving impossible to shake no matter how graceful Roman has always been about it—but because I don't want to even imagine being with anyone else, and I don't want Roman thinking like that either. And the thought of *Jakob* wanting me in that way, none of it is making any sense. It churns in my gut like spoiled meat.

"I don't get it," I say, trying to figure him out. "I know you're not the jealous type. I mean come on, what is he, thirty-five, at least? I'm literally half his age. Where's all this coming from?"

"I don't know," he says, frustrated by the whole thing. "Just forget it." He pulls me toward him, closing his eyes and sinking his face into my neck, wanting to escape inside me, to get away from those horrible feelings.

"Tell me," I whisper. "I want to know."

He doesn't want to answer, but he does. "It's a feeling I have, okay? It's a strong feeling. Eve, it makes my skin crawl. It scares me to no end." He looks at me with unblinking eyes, his hand gently brushing the hair away from my face. "I want to protect you, and he's … I don't know how to explain it, but he's a big threat—to you and to us. I know it. And *knowing* things the way I always do, the way Phoenix and I both do, it's becoming much rarer."

"You didn't tell me that," I say, not attempting to mask my surprise and concern. Cian's death left humanity on autopilot, and now Roman is losing his ability too. It's like we have been abandoned.

"Yeah. It started when you were, you know … for all those weeks."

"Oh," I say, feeling strangely guilty. Knowing there has to be a price to pay for this unearthly love.

"It's not your fault, obviously. It's just, I think I was so concerned, so connected to what was going on in this lifetime that I began to lose touch with, you know, wherever it is that it all comes from."

That strikes me as absolutely my fault, no matter how he struggles to phrase it otherwise.

"And what about our lives together?" I ask.

"I've forgotten most of those now too. They started fading the second you came back to yourself. Along with everything I've spent my life knowing, the things I came in with, the memories of all my lives, the past lives of other people, and the knowing I used to depend on, it's all been fading slowly, like a long sunset."

The next day Roman goes away with Jakob.

They leave before sunrise. Jakob comes into his room to get him, unannounced, waking us both with a loud clap of his hands and the news that it is time for Roman to begin training for his new job. I pull the sheets up to my chin, trying to will our uninvited guest to turn around—or even better, to leave, neither of which he does.

And a few minutes later I watch from Roman's window as Jakob leads him along with a few others to a large helicopter pad just beyond the gardens. They are an informal-seeming group, a handful of tall, strong boys around our age, all Sages, and a few adult men, all darkly robed Dragon souls, one of whom is Rasuil of the Aion Dorea, who, along with Ansel and Sourial, I don't trust.

Where they go and what they are doing is anyone's guess. But they don't come back for three days.

"So, what's this new job?" I ask, finally sitting across from Roman at dinner after three long days without him. He's just gotten back. His eyes are bloodshot, and he hasn't taken a bite from his plate. He doesn't seem to be able to explain the new job. He doesn't seem to be able to say anything at all.

The longer he sits quietly, struggling for words, the more worried I feel.

"It's your favorite," I say of the tender roast beef and soft salty potatoes he's pushing around with his fork. The food at Antiquus is always out of this world, second only to the opulent candlelit dining room we get to eat it in, every meal a feast in this lavish, abundant kingdom—where the person I love sits before me, seemingly unable to form a sentence.

"Resource collection trips," Roman finally says in a cold affectionless tone of the new job that will take him away for two to three nights at least once a week.

"That's what they're called? I mean, officially? Resource collection trips? What exactly are you collecting?"

These excursions don't sit right with me. For one thing, no one seems to think much of it, like they're on some kind of mundane paper route not worth discussing. But no one can tell me what the job entails or where it was they've gone.

"There's no official name," he says. "That's just what we call them."

But everything has an official name. Everything is slapped with a label, but not this? It doesn't make sense, though I can see he's ready to talk about something else. So I let it go, coaxing him back with boring tales of my adventures in biology and genetic engineering.

He smiles a bit here and there, but he never fully loses that look he had when he walked in, the shell-shocked, traumatized, distracted stare.

After a few hours pass, Roman seems a little more relaxed. At least his shoulders have dropped down away from his ears. So I consider asking him again as we sit outside in wooden Adirondack chairs, watching the aurora borealis in the brisk winter air, the neon green northern lights rolling and dancing across the starry sky.

"What's wrong? You're so quiet." But he just smiles his

most genuine loving smile and kisses my hand, which he's been holding, trying hard to reassure me that everything is fine, all the while knowing that I'm not fooled.

By morning, he's almost completely back to himself and is absolutely normal by the end of the day. Then they leave again that night.

It goes on like this for weeks.

Through sheer grit, he manages to make the depression he's slipping into barely noticeable, but I can still see it. It's always there, like the tiniest pebble in his shoe, barely detectable but throwing off his gait nonetheless. Over time I can tell that the burden is getting more difficult to bear, the weight of it slowly crushing his soul, though he still refuses to tell me much of anything.

Weeks later, I've finally had enough.

It's before day, maybe 4:30, when Roman crawls into his bed, curling his ice-cold body into the fetal position. They always come and go at irregular hours, which I'm now certain is done intentionally. But it doesn't matter because I've been awake all night.

"I want to know exactly what you do out there," I say. "Where you're at and what you're doing." My voice is as scared as it's firm. I'm scared he won't tell me and scared that he will.

"Eve," he says, gravely and hoarse, "I'm so tired." His

gentle way of putting me off. Something he does all the time now.

A rush of tears well up in my eyes, and my cheeks turn hot.

Why can't he tell me? Why won't he? These questions crush my heart as I lie there. They make me doubt what we have really built in all these lifetimes and in this one. There's also the fear that there's another reason altogether, that he *can't* share it with me. That he isn't allowed to. Fear plus sadness and frustration and worry equal tears—a lot of tears. I sniffle and try to wipe them away as fast as they fall from my eyes.

He rolls away toward the wall, as if he's going to go to sleep as I lie next to him crying quietly, which we both know he'd never do. Has he done it before? Sure, plenty of times, during plenty of other lifetimes. But he'd never do it now.

A minute later, he rolls back toward me, covers his eyes with his arm, and then he begins to talk.

TWELVE

———— ✠ ————

"Everything's abandoned out there," he mumbles softly. "It's for the taking." He's talking from under his arm without looking, in a robotic "just to reassure me" voice.

I stay quiet. I deserve more. And he knows that.

I haven't gone "out there," not really, not beyond the hollow. But that tiny trifle of information even I have already heard. *Everything's abandoned out there; it's for the taking.* I've heard people say it here and there, of the world outside the walls of Antiquus. It sounds like nothing more than a line in script coming from Roman.

"We scavenge for things," he elaborates, still not looking at me.

"Like what? What could we possibly need here?"

Antiquus is a veritable kingdom of resources that won't be depleted for centuries—practically limitless food, water, weaponry, and fuel and the ability to make as much as we want of each. I know that. And he knows that I know that.

"Typically we go for trucks, eighteen-wheelers, grain, fuel, even airplanes. It's all just, you know ... out there." He sounds like a person standing on a ledge simultaneously threatening to jump and begging to be brought in.

"Who flies them? The airplanes?" I press him again, knowing he's lying and knowing that he needs me to.

As he lowers his arm, I see the tears rushing down his face, a raging river compared to my few frustrated drops.

"There are so many of them," he says, his eyes staring up at the ceiling. I know that this is the moment when the truth will begin.

And the truth is worse than anything I have imagined.

I struggle to process what Roman finally tells me his new job entails. Loading in the helicopter with the others and flying to the nearest airport, where semi-trucks are lined up for miles along the tarmac, all filled from top to bottom with human remains. They carry each body from the trucks, loading as many as a thousand at a time onto cargo planes, then flying to the Grand Canyon, descending to an altitude of about five thousand feet, opening the cargo doors and pushing the bodies out. It's a "joint effort" apparently. Primitus is doing the same thing. Roman says there are other planes, just like theirs, all dropping bodies from the sky.

"It looks like it's raining dead people," he says, utterly horrified. "Some of the ones from the other planes, I swear they are moving, flailing their arms as they fall. Did you know that you can dump every human on Earth into the Grand Canyon and it won't even come close to filling it up? All seven and a half billion of us would only create a tiny little pile," he explains with a vacant stare.

I'm ready to confront Jakob the next morning. He's come to see the advances we've been making in the biotech tower.

"This progress since you've gotten involved—it's inhuman. You really are pretty smart, huh?" he says with his trademark smile.

I just shrug and swipe my monitor to bring up a chart showing an anomaly I've found: that more than 97% of the people in Antiquus have Rh-negative blood, which is highly improbable. Strangely, he doesn't seem surprised.

"Statistically speaking, it's actually impossible," I say. "But before we get into this, I want to talk about Roman's new job. Listen, I understand we can't just leave all the dead lying around, but—"

"Over five hundred million dead, decaying, rotting corpses—no Eve, we can't just leave them lying around."

He can be so condescending. His moods have been proving impossible to predict. There's no rhyme or reason, no pattern at all that I can find.

"Yeah, Jakob, I get that, but—"

"Do you? You know, because sometimes I wonder." He swipes the monitor angrily, sending the images whirling past in a blur. "I have my doubts about you. Perhaps you're too sensitive to ever effectively lead. And look at what you're wearing. It's not appropriate."

"How so?" I ask. I happen to be wearing the clothes I wore the night I first came here—just jeans and a T-shirt. They make me comfortable—and I figure if I can go where I want, I certainly can wear what I want.

"Never mind," he says, clearly annoyed.

"But why Roman? At least tell me that."

"And there it is." He throws his hands up, shaking his head. "Your worst quality of all, Eve. You overanalyze *everything!*"

The room goes awkwardly silent as the twenty people I've been working with the last few days pretend to go about their research.

"He's young and able bodied. There's no big reason *why*, Eve. It just is what it is. The dead must be collected. Leaders have to make decisions, always for the greater good. Maybe when you learn to stop wondering about every little thing, second guessing, overthinking, you'll be ready for the enormous responsibility, the burden of leading us, which takes a focused and steady hand. But right now, you are *nowhere near* able to handle someone handing you that kind of power. When you've got the fate of humanity resting on your shoulders you can't go running off down every goddamn rabbit hole you come across!" There's scorn in his eyes and disgust. Like the plan for me to lead Aurora may need reevaluating. And like the Aion Dorea might just be wrong about me.

Then he storms out of the lab.

After a good three minutes, my shock wears off. I close my gaping mouth and sit down at my desk. I just sit there. Feeling a deep need to turn off my whirling mind, to shut out the useless ramblings of my wounded ego. That's the only way I know how to hear the faint whispers of my soul.

I'm ready to listen now, breathing deep and closing my eyes.

I hear Cian's words in my heart. *It's not the apocalypse that scares us.*

I go deeper into their meaning. Not the apocalypse. It's not the lifting of the veil that scares us. It's the cover-up that does. The truth is that there are no fish and no bees and no babies. There are huge problems with this world, problems that are too big, because this world is ending. Be honest.

That's what Cian was trying to tell me. The apocalypse is good if destruction is rebirth. It may be hard for people to let go. They'll feel their world crumbling down around them. But the truth is that it was never there. So let the lie be exposed. Don't shield people. Be unafraid, and never cover the truth. This world *is* falling away, and I'm not supposed to help to prop it up.

Cian was telling me in advance to work against the lies, and here I am working for them. It's time to move in another direction now.

Then the gentle tug of my soul tells me that there's something else. I listen, returning to the quiet to tune in again.

Wondering is more than just our sacred duty as humans.

It was one of the last things Cian ever said to me. He was standing in our little kitchen in the house on East Gate Drive handing me a slice of buttered toast. It was the day before he left for his final, fateful trip. The day before I started school for the first time, after which any semblance of life as I'd known it before would end. "It's not curing the disease," he said, "but wondering whether we should that is perhaps our noblest endeavor."

This is where the whispers of my soul have led me, back to the words of my grandfather—and what he went on to say next.

"We watch for signs that we're on the right path and signs

we're not. If you should ever discover that all the answers are always close at hand and you find yourself surrounded by a world more and more eager to give them to you, when wondering things and questioning things is discouraged—or worse, met with scorn, or ridiculed—that's when wondering becomes as important to human survival as oxygen. If you ever suspect you're working to cure the wrong disease, just wonder your way back. And the place to begin always is with wondering about ourselves."

I've wanted to revisit the remote location where I met the Aion Dorea, to talk with Bronwyn and Clio and Pythagoras too. So why haven't I?

Wondering is the breath of life, and it's time to start breathing.

As I stride past the aquifers, which I now know are being used to poison people with the diseases of complacency and compliance—while I've been working to clone grouper for them to eat in the future—I'm seething with anger. Legs marching, feet stomping, arms pumping through the tunnels. *Oh, you want to save the world, do you, Jakob? Well good luck, you fucking prick, let's see how far you get without my help. You treat me like a child, you idiotic bastard. Well, let me tell you something, I'm a grown woman. That's right, I am powerful and I know what I want, and it isn't to work on your projects, to save the world but let humanity disintegrate. No thank you. Don't underestimate me! Because it will be the worst mistake you ever made!*

My imaginary fight with Jakob is going quite well. He is cowering in the corner, and I am just about to really let him have it. When out of nowhere, I start crying instead—absolutely bawling my eyes out—and swinging a few sad punches.

I'm a sniveling blubbering mess, a mumbling wobbling fool, by the time I walk up to the wooden doors at the end of the long tunnel. They swing open, and there is Bronwyn with her arms outstretched.

She glows in her white robe as she sits across from me, holding my hands as I wail out every detail, everything that's happened since I saw her last, ping-ponging rapidly from one emotion to the next, from sad to wistful, from rage-fueled to scared and hopeless, from fiery and determined to helpless and confused. After a good thirty minutes, I take a breath and find that I'm already starting to feel better.

"Am I really some kind of queen?" I ask her, my first complete sentence, as she hands me another tissue.

"Yes," she confirms. "We have long thought this could be the case. Cian, of course, was always convinced, but it wasn't until you had your Animus test that your royal bloodline finally showed itself."

I let out a sigh.

"What is it?" she asks.

"I mean, I think I'm just getting really tired of people telling me what I am. Eve, the happy little island. Eve, the oldest soul on Earth. Eve, the flipping antichrist, a seductress sent to ensnare the innocent, some kind of Zodiac freak who sits all alone in a big dumb chair and sleeps in a crypt beneath the earth. I guess I just don't know what to actually believe. Teenage girls have a hard enough time figuring out who they are as it is."

"Is that right?" She smiles.

"Yes, that's right, we do. And people seem to tell me I'm something different every time I turn around."

I realize, but only after it's out of my mouth, that I'm complaining about being told I'm a *queen*. What a spoiled brat I must sound like.

"All labels are false," she says. "Identity politics used to made the infinity inside humanity small enough to manage."

My mouth drops open. How much I've been letting these lies shape my reality astonishes me. Who cares what people say I am? It doesn't matter. It isn't even real.

She nods knowingly. "It's one of the easiest things to forget. Yes, you are the only living person from a sacred and ancient royal bloodline, but ultimately, you are simply you. You are everything you have always been and everything you will ever be, right here and now. There is no label worthy of what we are." She brushes the hair from my face. "But it's true. There is a marker called Kayaamat in your blood."

"*Resurrection*," I breathe, translating the Hindu word. This must be why Shamus wants my blood. "My blood has the power to raise the dead?"

"Kayaamat is not what it seems," Pythagoras says as he walks into the room. "There have been five queens before you who've all had this marker. You are our sixth."

"Ever?" I ask.

"Yes," Pythagoras says gravely, and Bronwyn nods.

"All right," I say, approaching my wit's end with all of these enigmas wrapped in mysteries, "so, what *is* the real meaning?"

They just stare at me in silence—exactly what Cian would do if it were something I had to figure out on my own—and pissing me off in grand fashion.

I stand up and scream. Not at them, and not words of any kind, just a long, loud bloodcurdling scream. Which has positively zero effect on either of them.

"Here's what I think," I start ranting, "I don't think *anything* is what it seems. An apocalypse isn't the destruction of the world. Kayaamat isn't resurrection. You know what else? Aion Dorea doesn't mean 'faithful servants of humanity' either! But no one seems to be bothered by that fact, except me! But it's bothered me from the moment Ansel first said it. Because it was a lie, and I knew it was a lie. And now you've built *this* place, and Aurora, all on the premise of Animus being the remedy for *unexplained* celestial acts of aggression on an inherently flawed human race. This place is built on a lie. Shamus caused the events and the unthinkable, not God. I'm certain Cian knew that, and I'm sure you all know that too."

I start to pace, eyeing them as I do. "So why would 'faithful servants of humanity' lie to said humanity …" I'm looking around like a paranoid schizophrenic at the books on the shelves and at all the odd and interesting things on their desks, watching the two of them calmly staring at me …

Apocalypse is the opposite of what people think.

The meaning of Kayaamat is misleading.

My thoughts turn to the Aion Dorea. My eyes searching, I see strange clocks everywhere. On Bronwyn's desk, books on Galileo, Mayan astrology charts …

"You're something else altogether, aren't you?" I ask, then watch their reactions, how neither of them breaks eye contact with me. "You're keepers of some kind. That's it, isn't it? You're the keepers of an important secret—" The subtlest smile from each of them tells me it's true— "Some kind of forbidden knowledge … about time and about existence. All I'm wondering now is whether it's the all-important truth or the greatest lie ever told."

More silence from them forces me to look deeper.

I see a picture of the Zodiac on Bronwyn's desk. The round image catches my eye because it has thirteen signs, not twelve. Then I see it, hung in a golden frame on the wall over her desk.

It's the ancient Greek symbol for Ophiuchus.

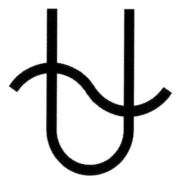

"You were the one who wanted the lunar calendar, weren't you?" I say to Bronwyn. "Because of Ophiuchus." She nods.

"She insisted," Pythagoras says.

"As did he," Bronwyn says, and they share a small smile.

"And Clio, right?" I guess, and they both nod. "But not

Ansel, Rasuil, or Sourial. They wanted to keep the solar calendar." Neither of them deny it, so I take that as confirmation of the divide between them that I've suspected. "But on what? And why?"

"The three of us," Pythagoras says, "along with three others in Primitus—Kali, Claudius, and Thea—believe we've entered into a window of time in which the awakening of humanity may occur. Ansel, Sourial, Rasuil, and the other three in Primitus don't agree."

"There *is* a war; it's already begun," Bronwyn says, "but, like most things, it's not what you think. It's not a brewing conflict between old and new souls. Yes, it's a war of souls, but it's between the enlightened and the unenlightened, and half of them are sleepwalking through the battle. There are only two weapons in this war, lies and the truth. We pushed for the lunar calendar because it is a reminder, helping people begin to remember. It points them toward the truth."

"Which is?" I press her for more.

"That, I'm afraid, I can't help you with. You've got to find it ... like each of the queens who came before you," she adds, another clue.

"Five queens before me ..." I start to think aloud, "I'm the sixth ... Ophiuchus, thirteen, the serpent bearer..." The dots are not connecting; nothing comes to mind.

"There is one thing we can show you …" Bronwyn says as Clio comes floating into the room.

"It's time, right?" Clio beams.

THIRTEEN

"Do you ever get the feeling Earth isn't your real home?"

It's a rhetorical question. One that, as she asks me, fills Clio's voice with fascination, makes her blue eyes sparkle, and her whole body light up, standing before me in the center of the mysterious library like a heavenly angel who's fallen to Earth. Then Clio tells me that none of us are from here, and that she is from the realm where we are headed to, an overworld called Kosmos.

"The highest overworld is Soteria," Clio says. "Kosmos is just one below that."

Just then, the giant dark ladders attached to the highest shelves begin to quake, clattering against the wood floor beneath them, making a shuddering sound that continues to increase until it's rattling my bones. Then the diamond-covered iceberg of a chandelier begins to tremble from the ceiling down, the chain shaking first, then the crystals clashing as they flail about, sending light prisms dancing in dizzying circles on every wall and splashing rainbow spectrums, bold red and green streaks of light all around us.

"Down on Earth," Clio says, "we're just visitors in a foreign place. We are like eagles exploring the bottom of the sea. It's interesting here, yes, but we are displaced nonetheless." She closes her eyes as she continues to speak, centering herself. "If we get too involved, too attached, then we completely forget …"

She falls silent, seeming to go deeper into her meditation, the quaking walls rattling harder now, sending books raining down from their shelves.

"Forget what?" I ask.

"That we come from the stars," Clio says, her eyes shooting open. She looks concerned, like this is something I should know. "This is not our home, Eve. "We are *souls*, not humans. We are the light inside our bodies. That light is who and what we are—celestial beings of the one light and love and of infinite expansion. We are not separate from one another nor are we separate from the one source of all life. We choose to go behind these eyes, each time where, as we learn and experience, the universe becomes conscious of itself, but we are limited by nothing …"

Clio's long blond hair turns to a short black pixie cut,

her pale skin into a deep bronze, and her blue eyes change to a warm caramel brown. "We are infinitely powerful sources of consciousness crammed, *temporarily*, into these small dense bodies."

Her now dark hair grows down past her shoulders, then turns red and curly, and her eyes transform to a blazing green. Then, just as swiftly, she morphs back to herself. "Skin, hair, how we look, it's all an illusion, along with the story of who you are, the story others tell you, and the one you tell yourself. You must surrender it all in order to move higher. You must free yourself from the illusion."

Clio's voice trails off, and her head starts tipping back, her neck relaxing, sending her face toward the violently shaking chandelier.

"Unlike traveling to Eremis," she drones, trancelike, "which is the first overworld to Earth, one small realm away, as easy as slipping behind a curtain, reaching Kosmos is more challenging. It takes more focus."

"Got it," I say. I'm more ready than ever to shed my identity, all the layers of illusion this world is heaping on me, and just as eager to see what it is that I will be shown. Before I even close my eyes, I feel the vibration, not from the floor, which is strangely still despite the rattling walls and ceiling, but from inside me. Like the violent shaking of a rocket leaving the atmosphere, my astral body is parting from my flesh, preparing to travel farther than ever before.

When I focus all my attention in the center of my forehead with the intent to go beyond Eremis, the crushing pressure starts, millions of tons of pressure pushing down on my head, face, and bones. Trying to propel upward, to ascend through it, is like trying to swim toward the sky through a crashing wave.

"Keep going; you're at the edge," I hear Clio's voice call to me from somewhere above. "Eremis extends as far as the winds blow and the clouds float through the sky and contains all the wilderness, both around us and inside us. Focus, transcend yourself to go beyond that realm."

The burning in my forehead turns to a searing blaze. Suddenly my heart seems to fly out of my chest, and everything changes.

I've never realized how heavy the environment is on both Earth and Eremis, like I've been unknowingly breathing water my whole life. The dense air begins to thin, easing the pressure until it fully dissolves. Then a force starts pulling me up. I ascend rapidly through the four realms between Eremis and Kosmos, each one revealing itself to me fully as I pass through it in the blink of an eye.

The first is Vana. The holy forest, the realm of wood and magic, where I look out at timber-covered mountains, stand in groves of aspen trees, and float above dense thickets of evergreen. Its inhabitants are workers of light, spiritual mediums, and all types of healers, mystical and magical beings able to directly intervene with life on Earth. They touch the lives of humans who are unaware that the person before them is an ascended being interacting with them while standing firmly in another realm. Only dogs and other animals can tell the difference.

Next comes Hydras, the blessed waters. This realm is where poetry and music and literature and art come from; it's the home of Pythagoras. Where all types of muses flit in and out of Earth, felt but unseen. Artists, who the blessed beings identify at birth, can connect with this realm. Musical rhythms flow through the air like floating streams, light rains, and torrential downpours fall on seas and ponds and puddles, forming different beats and secret coves where muses mill about on ancient rocks covered with climbing flower vines. The songs echo through the grotto caves, where deep inside, images float in the reflection of the protected waters, from the epic *Iliad* to the sculpture of David.

Aura, the divine sky, is the home of Bronwyn, where winged horses carry angels and deities like her between massive floating rock formations. A strong vibration reverberates through me, like striking a tuning fork inside your soul, which I realize are prayers. A constant buzz of prayers and intentions, thought and spoken by humans on Earth, waft upward through the thin crisp air, each one like its own invisible radio wave that I can tune in to hear.

Nakara, the sacred golden city, is a palatial shining kingdom where the shimmering streets are washed in peace, and where a blanket of serenity enwraps the whole of the city and all who dwell here. As I stand before a palace of gold, I learn that we have gold within our bodies, a small amount of gold in our blood, and that it's a constant reminder of Nakara and a connection to this place, home to the ascended masters, from Confucius and Buddha to all the saints and archangels who move freely through all the realms above and below, stirring hearts, awakening souls, and connecting the earthly with the divine.

I'm staring at the back of a man sitting on a golden bench, an old man, when a shooting star streaks by. I turn to watch it and find myself in Kosmos, the celestial realm of stars. Turning back, the golden city is gone, and so is the man.

I look out into the vacuum of deep space. Clio flies by, racing toward a neon green nebula, and I follow after her. My vision ebbs and flows, in and out and back and forth, like my irises have turned to Slinkys. I can see in light-years, I realize. To my right are swirling clusters of galaxies and other universes. To my left, the way the darkness moves like vapor, I know I'm seeing time and the dimensions of all realities, where instead of stars, there are *eyes*. They stretch on and on, eclipsing infinity. I stop to stare at it, the celestial wave of the space-time continuum tugging at me, pulling me in. Not with physical gravity but with the gravity in my soul.

I think of Clio, and she's beside me.

This way, I speak from my consciousness directly into hers. And her smile is like the sun as we head into the vapor, shooting across the galaxy toward Alpha Ophiuchi, a binary star, the brightest in the constellation of Ophiuchus. There is no passage of time or actual travel involved, nor any need to discuss where we're going. We simply arrive, floating before the bright yellow fireball with a ring of circumstellar dust encircling it like the slowly revolving wheel of a bicycle.

There are ancient gods and goddesses all around us, celestial beings of pure consciousness, who we don't see physically anywhere among the stars but who we feel by their presence.

Like lucid dreaming while wide awake as I stare at the star before me, somewhere else in my mind, geometric shapes in psychedelic colors begin folding and flowering, like a kaleidoscope that's teaching me things about the meaning of life. I hear a melodic female voice rising and falling in a singsong wave of notes—an ancient language, she tells me, one that I know very well.

I sit up choking and gasping for air, my eyes darting around the dark room.

The same way I always wake up with the same dream, only this time the lingering images of Cian, the frigid water, the lost nightstand, and Jude's face don't last long. I know not to worry about any of that yet. My head is full of other more pressing information. I've received a celestial download, a cosmic data dump, and a two-step plan.

Bronwyn sits by the bedside, holding a glass of water. I realize I'm not in my room or in Roman's.

Not only have I come to know and understand the seven overworld realms in a perfect and complete way, but now I also have full awareness of the seven underworld realms, in one of which there is something I need—in Haima, the first underworld, as close and as easy to slip into as Eremis. The desolate city of bloodshed, the storage place of all our base fears.

I stand on a wide deserted street in an abandoned industrial city, windless, yet my hair blows wildly. I hold out my hand. Then, watching my palm, I carefully select what I need as options appear—chemicals, drugs, diseases, plagues, one after the next at a rapid-fire pace.

I am there and back in less than the blink of an eye. Looking as if they've just appeared there by magic, I return with two vials in my hand, ones that Bronwyn recognizes right away. A virus called Soros, Greek for "coffin," a deadly ancient plague for which there has never been a cure.

"Are you sure you know what you're doing," she asks, her face expressionless, eyes floating from the long thin vials up to meet mine.

"I'm sure," I reassure her, and I am. This has to be brought in. It's a part of the Akashic records, which I now read like an audiobook plugged into my brain.

It's time for step two.

"Just relax," she says, offering me the water. "Rest here as long as you need."

"I've got to go." I tear the sheets off.

"I'll show you out," she stands, helping me up, and we both head for the door.

The vials securely tucked deep in my pocket, I run. As I sprint to the technology tower, my head feels light and clear and my mind quiet, inactive.

I find Rafe, Collins, and Seth sitting at the large round computer terminal, all hacking away.

"Can I?" I ask Collins. He gets up and I quickly sit down.

"What are you doing?" Seth rolls his chair over, peeking at the screens.

"Code breaking, want to help?" I ask, sifting rapidly through data on the shape and dimensions of Orion and Ophiuchus, on the Bible, Kabbalah, the Gnostic Gospels, and through images from ancient Egyptian symbols to da Vinci's *Vitruvian Man*, through theorems and symphonies. When I see Einstein's general theory of relativity, I stop.

Cocking my head to one side, I begin to see something. Then the numbers float off the screen toward me, rearrange themselves, and then become letters, words, in the ancient language of Tamil.

And it reveals a bold statement. One I struggle to understand.

"What?" Seth asks, desperate to know what I'm seeing. But it can't be right.

"Nothing," I lie, moving on to maps of ley lines covering the world.

"What code are you trying to break?" Rafe asks. "The origin of the universe?" he says to Seth and Collins, but neither one laughs as they study me.

"The Aion Dorea," I start, then see their confused faces. "They're basically the real-life Illuminati. A clandestine shadow government controlling everything, holding the fate of humanity in their hands."

"So, that's real?" Collins asks, stunned.

"Yeah," I say. "Very real."

"We were right ..." Rafe says, amazed.

"I think I'm going to pass out," Collins says.

"What do they want? World domination? Ruling elite? Slave class?" Rafe asks, assuming it's somehow them against us.

"They are in charge of our sleep," I say.

"Our *sleep*?" Rafe asks. "No, that's too boring. *Unless*, they control our dreams. And control us through our dreams!"

"They are in charge of our conscious awareness," I reframe. But no one seems to be catching on, so I elaborate while continuing to process the texts and images that I search: "We're otherworldly beings, all of us. We're not terrestrial, we're *celestial*. We're here to learn *something*, and that's what I've got to figure out."

"The meaning of life ..." Rafe's face is skeptical.

"Well, it sounds really hard when you say it like that! But, yes, I need to sort of boil down what this existence we are living now is all about. We're here to learn something very specific, and in order for us to learn it, we must walk a human experience. But remember, we're divine, so in order for us to walk a human experience, we must be kept in a state of illusion or sleep. And it's the Aion Dorea whose job it is to keep us asleep so we can feel and hurt and be human enough to learn this mysterious lesson. And they also must determine if and when our awakening can no longer be held back—when this lesson has run its course. Six of the members are of the opinion that humanity should still be kept in the illusion, and that it's their duty to continue doing the things they do in order to keep us asleep, while six others feel all the signs are indicating that the time has come." I say this knowing that I'm the deciding factor, whether I can solve the riddle of the purpose of this existence.

No pressure.

"So, this Aion Dorea has twelve members?" Rafe asks.

"Technically, now they have thirteen," I say, referring to myself. Seth starts fanning Collins.

"She's basically in the Illuminati," Collins whispers.

"I know, buddy, I know," Seth replies.

"You know how my grandfather could wake the dead?" I ask Rafe, knowing he was at the service and heard Jakob's story.

"I feel like you should definitely be in our club," Seth says—the weirdoes of the weirdoes.

"I think maybe you're our leader," Collins speculates, staring at me.

"There's a lot of that going around," I mumble.

"So, your dead-waking grandpa … he dies, and …" Rafe

waves his hand, prompting me to explain the connection.

"Since no one else has this ability, it's a sign—because there's always someone who can wake the dead, fate being subject to chaos and all. So, when there's not a waker anymore, it's a sign that this epoch is coming to an end. One of a few signs," I add, not wanting to go into the whole ancient royal bloodline Queen of the Aion Dorea thing.

"It's a sign of *what*, exactly?" Collins asks. "I'm sorry, are we supposed to be able to follow along here, because I've got literally nothing. It's like a blank sheet of loose leaf behind my eyes right now."

"It's time for the next awakening," Seth tells him.

"Exactly," I say, "The Lumerians, the Atlanteans, the ancient Egyptians, the Maya, and the ancient Greeks, these were the other five times in human history when this kind of window arrived, and large numbers of humans who could see through the illusion, who'd figured out what the meaning of that existence was, were no longer held back in this dimension. And now it looks like the time has come for the sixth. But I have to figure out *what* we need to awaken to. What's the greatest lie ever told ..." I say, typing and searching and growing increasingly frustrated.

"That cell phones don't cause cancer!!" Collins suggests with great enthusiasm. We all know they do—and no one is telling us!"

Seth shakes his head. "That's not it."

"Just ask your friends in the Illuminati!" Rafe suggests, very seriously, like I maybe hadn't thought of that.

"I have to crack the code," I say. "That's how it works. They can't even help. It's not their job. It's mine. Apparently, 'nothing good ever happens when they interfere with it.' At least that's what the giant serpent mother told me."

"What?" Collins asks, eyes wide, like he's not sure how much more he can take before his head flies off.

"Never mind. She also told me that humanity is going one way or the other; they are going up or they are going down, the course is set, and the window for ascent is short."

"Ascent … You mean the fifth dimension?" Rafe asks, stunned.

I nod. "That's exactly what I mean."

"Oh my god," Rafe breathes, "it's all happening. We're going to the fifth dimension," he marvels, then starts wandering around in a stupor.

Collins passes out cold.

As Seth fans him, I'm staring at the constellation Ophiuchus … something about it is calling me.

"What is it?" Rafe asks as I focus on the stars. I turn the image ninety degrees.

"It's a map!" I say, imposing a transparent image of

North America on top. I point to a dot on the right side of the screen. "There's Antiquus." And then to a dot on the left. "There's Primitus."

Then Rafe points to the top-left corner. "What's up there? In the northernmost tip of the continent …"

"Burrow, Alaska," I say with a very strong feeling, given my latest recurring dream, that that dot is Cian's nightstand.

"And there? The dot in between Antiquus and Primitus … the one that lines up perfectly with in the geographic center of North America …"

"Rugby," I whisper. What on earth is going on in Rugby?

FOURTEEN

—— ✠ ——

Jakob doesn't go with Roman and the others, who've left the day before on another mysterious "resource collection trip," otherwise known as "the crushing of Roman's soul via the dumping of the dead."

The reason I know that Jakob stayed behind is because he's in my room when I arrive in search of Cian's will, which for some reason has occurred to me that it may be some kind of key to a cipher. I burst through the door, heading for the armoire where it's stashed, and startle Jakob as he stands there reading it.

"What are you doing in here?" I demand, breathless from my run, yet so boldly that I surprise even myself.

"I could ask you the same thing," he chides, like I just walked in on him in his own room. "Do you *ever* sleep in here?" He lets out a little huff and slightly shakes his head.

"You know you're not supposed to read that," I say, growing worried as he walks toward me with Cian's will in his hands, feeling smaller the closer he gets, like somehow he is growing while I shrink.

"According to…"

"You were there. According to the Aion Dorea."

"According to Pythagoras," Jakob says. "You see, some of them are worth listening to. And some of them … eh, not so much." He's looming over me now. "Eve, tell me, why do I get the feeling that you're messing with things you shouldn't be?"

"Such as?" I ask, trying hard to keep my voice steady. As if there's a vortex that surrounds him—the closer he is, the more I get knocked off kilter. And as he stares down into my eyes, I even start to feel dizzy.

"What we are doing here, Eve, has taken Shamus and I *years* of planning." His teeth clench and his eyes fill with rage. "And your meddling and your disrespect will not be tolerated!" He whips the back of his hand across my face, sending me stumbling back.

"You have a very important role to play," he says, suddenly calm and composed as I retreat until I bump against the bed. "Don't worry, we didn't forget about you. Your role is critical—that part's true." He caresses my shoulder. "But it's not what you think it is," he whispers in my ear. "It's not *because* of you but *through* you. Through the secret Queen of the Aion Dorea that the next generation will arrive on Earth."

He moves his hand on top of my breast and squeezes it hard. "You and your sacred royal bloodline, and me, the chosen one, the resurrected. Through us," he says, licking his lips moving his mouth closer to mine. "There's a very good reason why there are no more pregnancies. It's quite obvious, actually. It's time to start over, and you and I are the new Adam and Eve."

Just then I think of the vials in my pocket, one of which I planned to eventually use on Jakob when I got the chance, when he could be isolated.

"Fuck off," I say.

"How dare you," he seethes. He pushes me onto the bed and throws himself on top of me, one arm easily pinning both of mine over my head. He slides his other hand slowly and roughly down my body. Feeling me all the way down to the waist of my jeans.

As he rubs his palm between my legs, he notices something deep inside my pocket. "What's this?" he asks, feeling around liberally before pulling it out.

He bites the cap off. "I was right, you have been up to something," his menacing whisper terrorizing as he brandishes the syringe at me.

"Don't, Jakob, stop," I say, feeling my weakness, my inability to fight him off, to stop anything he wants to do, and feeling his own power. Drowning in it.

"Soros ..." he reads on the vial. "My Greek is a bit rusty but might that mean ... ashes, or bones..." He moves the gleaming sharp needle toward my neck. I struggle against his grip, tears falling down my cheeks.

"Please," I beg him, feeling the cold metal pressing into my flesh.

"You know Shamus was right about you, Eve." He shakes his head. "You just don't know your place..." He tosses the vials to the floor and starts unbuckling his belt. "Always tempted to eat the apple from the tree and never *ever* to be trusted."

When people you love die right in front of you, time does strange things.

It can shrink or stretch, even bend.

And sometimes, depending on fate or the forces of the universe or maybe just which way the wind is blowing, these little pockets of space can be created. Rarer than black holes, stranger than vortexes, they're the eighth wonder of the world, the only places on Earth where certain things, impossible to see under ordinary circumstances, can be revealed—*the very things written on your soul.*

It happened to me, a split-second after I knew Cian was gone. I experienced one of these pauses in the ever-weaving fabric of the eternal, a momentary interruption in the broadcast. It was triggered, I think, by the anger at Shamus that had finally detonated inside me as full-blown mind numbing rage.

The same second I knew Cian was dead I felt a shift—the sudden realization that this life was nothing more than a slideshow. One second I was as deeply entrenched in the world as I'd ever been, head whirling, heart stunned, sweat covering my body, rage boiling in my veins … and the next second, I wasn't. I wasn't even where I'd been—standing on the dunes of Eremis watching death take my grandfather from me. I was in a stark white place, a place where nothing was happening at all. Where I felt blank and calm, fully detached from the trauma I'd just been enduring.

The first thing I noticed was a kind of quiet like I'd never heard before. It was utter and total, an airless sound. The silence went so deep that I could hear myself being alive. I could hear my pulse pounding on my temples like snare drums. I could hear the swooshing of air as it swirled through my lungs, even the light rustling of my hair as it grew.

Then out of the silent stillness, something began to crystalize before me—or rather *someone*. It was Roman, a projection of him. Surrounded by brilliant light, his eyes sparkled, his face and body was as calm and as relaxed as usual. He smiled at me, and though I was aware this wasn't really him, it felt the same as if it were. Then the light around him began to grow dimmer, and I started seeing something else, What lives just on the other side of his effortless smile and disarming eyes, his cool and breezy disposition. It was his darkness—his shadow side. The tortured depth that lives in him, that is just as much a part of him. I saw it as much with my eyes as I did with my heart. A profound and heavy place he had no plans of ever allowing me to see, I saw it then so easily. Brooding and intense, and cut into him like a ravine, it's part of what makes him seem much older than seventeen—because he is, in every sense of the word. With an almost unfathomable deepness carved into his soul over centuries, excavated by the scars of agonizing pain and the torture of great loss, blasted out by fiery bursts of incredible joy and eroded by a vast understanding of love and beauty.

All of this had been written on my own soul all along, and seeing it then was a feeling stranger than suddenly remembering your own name.

Also on my soul was that this wasn't the first lifetime where he remembered all his others; he'd always been this way. My soul had known that all along, though every other part of me had been completely unaware.

Then I was shown *why* he'd been hiding this dark powerful streak, why he wants to hide it still, because it runs right through him and leads straight to me. His darkness touches my own, and I saw then how it encircles us, how it has been there since the day we met. I realized that it's what I'd been unconsciously feeling all along, pulling me toward him—like the dark pull of gravity that binds galaxies together.

I watched as our souls swirled and twisted together in a mystifying and secret conversation—where mine understood this place as part of his, along with my part in it, as only I could, and he knew that I did.

A wisp of pale yellow light suddenly billowed before me where Roman had been, an angel of sorts, whose radiant warmth traveled through me. *From this place alone will your love become real.* She spoke right into me, her heart conversing directly with mine.

For all of those lifetimes our love hasn't been real? I asked in response.

It's only been as real as you were capable of creating. I'm here to give you a glimpse of the highest form of human love that exists. You'll still have to discover it for yourself in this life. Whether you will is up to you. But it's finally possible, through you and Roman, for this love to be brought to Earth. This love is truth. It's whole. It's the dark and the light. One untainted by fear of the other.

Her thoughts entered through my head softly, like choir bells, but grew into a mighty echo as they moved down toward my heart, until I felt the whole universe and everything in it, all somehow inside my chest, infusing me with so much space and so much energy and so much light it burned like a wildfire and hurt to contain.

Real love isn't meant to be held in. Breathe it out, Eve. And with a mighty exhale—what looked like the sun exploding from my mouth and my chest—a warm life-giving glow consumed the entire mysterious blank place. I knew this feeling was Roman's love for me and my love for him—I recognized it, but my soul had never experienced it like this before.

This is the purest human love to exist in the universe. It's the oldest and most complete, the love you and Roman are capable of. From the moment you met in this lifetime, it was being held back, kept at bay—from both of you, though his was harder to contain—so events could unfold, so you were able to forge your deep connection with Jude, so you could love him. Fate depends on it.

If falling in love with Jude was like butterflies in my head as I soared through the clouds, airy and light, then the love Roman and I share is an atomic bomb. It obliterates everything in its path.

It's immortal love that defies things like space and time.

That laughs at death and sails on comets. And once it's brought into the flesh, once it pierces my heart outside this strange place, once it's fully manifested on Earth, there's no going back. It would have been futile to try to stop it from ravaging fate's plans.

Our love is stronger than even the plans of fate.

I wake to the taste of blood.

Swallowing hard several times gets it out, for the most part. The throbbing in my cheekbone and the burning between my legs don't go away so easily. I roll onto my side and wince. I touch the inside of my thighs, which are hot and bruised, and see that my wrists are no better.

Sitting up onto my elbows sends a fresh batch of new pains ricocheting through me. Hanging on my armoire is a long heavy cloak—and beside me, a note:

"Maybe you should start wearing this."

Letters swirling and neat on the fine card stock, it has the twisted feeling of a romantic gift from my private monster.

Wanting to search for the vials, I try to climb out of the bed. I fall to the ground with a thud and hiss of pain. Not surprisingly, the deadly vials are nowhere to be found. I crawl to my jeans, a rumpled pile flung to the corner of the room, gritting my teeth against the searing pain I feel all over my body. After searching the pockets just to be sure, I finally accept that they're gone, in the hands of Jakob now. I drop my jeans down into my lap, in part to cover the bruises all along my inner thighs.

Jakob left Cian's will laying on the floor next to the bed. I crawl over to it and begin rolling it back up.

There's a light knock on my door, and I instantly start shaking.

"Eve," Seth whispers through the door.

"I'm here," I say, my voice hoarse from the screams that Jakob's hand stifled. The door opens, and after taking a half-second to digest what has happened, Seth rushes to grab a blanket off my bed and gently wraps it around my bruised and naked body.

"We started to worry when all the cameras leading to your room were deactivated," he says, regret and remorse and anger and sadness all hanging like swinging nooses in his voice. "I tried to get down here earlier, but the tunnel was heavily guarded all night."

"I couldn't stop him," I cry, hearing my own shock.

"Eve, look at me," he says. "There was nothing you could do. He's more than twice your size."

His tender words send a river of tears rushing down my face. "But I know how to fight," I mutter. "I just couldn't … he …"

Seth looks lost for words—or for in how to frame something he feels he needs to say.

"What?" I ask, though I fear that he's about to tell me some awful thing about myself.

"Listen, Eve ... I really don't care if you're the best goddamn fighter, or what ..." He trails off, struggling to find a way to articulate what he's attempting to say. "You're only alive right now because he decided not to kill you."

"What?" I breathe, struggling to understand why he's saying this. I already feel defenseless enough.

"Eve, if we're being totally honest ... I mean, I could kill you right now. Any man can hurt, overpower, even kill any woman really, at any moment. That's just ... it's a fact." He shakes his head. "It's something that we know, us men, in a very primal part of us ... I am so sorry he hurt you, that he chose to do that."

I understand that he's trying to help me, and he understands that what he wants to articulate is something difficult. I nod. And we silently agree to move on.

"Rugby, that's where I need to go," I say after a minute of silence. "I'm going to steal the helicopter. As soon as it's back."

"It is back," he says.

"So Roman's back?" My voice sinks, and tears well up again, both at the thought of knowing what Jakob did and what it will do to Roman tearing into me and my desperation to be in his arms.

"He came back with the others a couple of hours ago," Seth says, "but he's gone again."

"Gone? Where?"

Seth studies me. He's gauging my mental stability, or lack thereof.

"I'm fine! Just, what? What is it?" I erupt.

Seeing that he's got no other choice, Seth takes out a tablet, one that's been heavily modified from its original standard-issue state, and starts a video.

It's footage from the landing pad. I see the usual group hop down from the helicopter, but then Jakob enters from the other side of the frame. He greets Roman, pulling him in and whispering something in his ear. Roman's already pained expression is abruptly overrun by shock and incomprehension.

Then I see the vial in Jakob's hand as he raises it up from his side and Roman's unsuspecting face not seeing what I see.

"No," I whisper, looking away from the screen, burying my eyes in my hands. When I force myself to look back, the helicopter has taken off and is flying away.

My sobs start instantly but take time to become heard. For a good minute my unrelenting wailing is breathless and silent. All inhale. All convulsions. Seth shields himself over me. It's a hug, but it does no more to protect me than it would against a spray of bullets. And that's an appropriate thought: I feel like I've just been gunned down.

PART THREE

SALT

FIFTEEN

—— ✠ ——

The ax feels good in my hands.

It feels lighter and lighter the more I swing it. With every slice and every chop, each time it smashes through another log I breathe out a huge huff, a white cloud of excruciating pain flinging out of me and into the world.

Roman has been given a lethal dose of the virus I planned to use on Jakob. I know the effects of Soros. I've died from it before. Death will come slowly and painfully. It will start with a single cough, but I will not allow myself to think of how it will end.

Sweat pouring off me in the dead of winter, dripping down my neck and flinging off my brow with each crushing blow I deliver. There's a wildfire inside me. What Jakob's done to Roman and to me … it's a monstrous blaze now, and it's burning my insides down to charred ruins.

And there's something else on my mind, or rather in my heart. The message I saw embedded in Einstein's theory and whether or not it's the first half of the code. I'm struggling to accept it, now more than ever. The words it revealed. Words that my heart won't let my mind absorb: that there is no good or evil. How can that possibly be?

The ax falls to rest at my side as I pant, staring straight ahead at a tree I haven't noticed before.

Half in curiosity, half instinct, I walk out of the hollow, farther away from Antiquus, farther into no man's land. The tree is as tall as it is wide and covered in soft green leaves, a beam of golden yellow light illuminating it from all sides. Strange yellow fruit hangs from its branches, like large oblong lemons but bigger, brighter, and with bumpier skin. *It's a citron tree.* Here in the Adirondack forest, covered with deciduous leaves and bearing fruit in the dead of winter… I sigh. Maybe I've lost it again. Checking back out because it's more than I can handle—raped by Jakob and seeing Roman murdered, a murder that I brought upon him.

This tree is about as real as Ansel's lizard eyes, I think as I collapse to my knees at the base of it. Then I slump over, hands in the mud and snow, my body convulsing with a torturous mixture of bitter anger and utter sorrow.

One of the long yellow citrons lays on the ground next

to me. Picking it up, vividly feeling its texture, I know I'm heading back to the dark side. Only this time, I may be going in even deeper, and with Roman gone, there won't be anyone to keep me alive. Rolling the long bumpy fruit in my hand, I realize that I don't care. All I want is to surrender. I want to die.

So I lie down on the cold wet earth, hugging the fruit into my chest with both hands, one ear to the ground. I close my eyes, though tears continue to rain through my matted lashes. It seems like my weeping is the only sound in the whole forest; the rest is silence and stillness.

Even though I'm lying in the snow, I start to feel warm, a warmth that slows my breathing from choppy panicked gasps to a calm and measured rhythm. Soon my heart rate follows, from a wild pounding drum to a strong and constant thud.

Light is all I see behind my eyes, stunning and piercing, diamond white brilliance—I am the light and it is me—something I know and accept all at once. Then the light dissolves. The world is nothing and all is quiet. Then, rising up out of the earth beneath me like a coiled cobra, I see darkness. Like space billowing up in spirals of black clouds, engulfing me. It's a powerful force, destructive and menacing, yet it's as beautiful as the light, and it's also me. The darkness is one and the same with me and with the light.

The pain inside my chest begins to change. It turns into anger, and then the anger morphs into rage, then into merciless vengeance.

The rage and the vengeance course through me like tar in my veins, thick and heavy. Wrath so powerfully dark it feels superhuman. I watch it creep across my heart, a slick of black mercury spreading, engulfing, supercharging me with fury until it meets the light. When the darkness touches the light, I feel my heart sync with the perfection of the universe. I feel complete. Whole. For the first time in my life, or maybe ever, I am fully here, awake and alive and whole. It all makes perfect sense now—especially what Seth was trying to tell me earlier.

My eyes snap open. The tears are gone.

My feet pound heavy on the earth through the forest clearing. Looking at the sprawling fortress before me, everything is crisp, sharp, and focused—there is only one thought in my mind.

It's time to wake the sleeping dragon.

I stalk through the towering bronze gates, my ax resting ready on my shoulder. I search for Jakob. I hunt him like prey. And he's remarkably easy to find. In the great hall, his legs crossed, face unsuspecting as he sits with his high council, hoarding power.

Mouths gaping, the seven of them watch me enter from the opposite side of the mammoth hall.

With every stride, the wet rubber bottoms of my boots squeak across the shiny wood floor, snow covered and half-laced.

Muddy hands, matted hair, busted face, and bloodstained T-shirt. A cool river running though my veins, deep blue water with crimson fire blazing across the surface.

"I never could find my bra," I announce very loudly. "You don't have it, do you, Jakob?" I ask, monotone, expressionless, searing him with my stare, the iron ax slung over my shoulder like a baseball bat. I relish a moment in the terror on his face, the humiliation brought upon him. I relish him having to sit there and witness what I am—wild, dangerous, pure light and total darkness, fragile and indestructible all at once.

"If this is about Roman being sent back to Primitus, it was because we found out he's actually a new soul," Jakob says, and all I see is the huge web of lies he lives in. What a tangled sad mess it is. And that Roman was right; Jakob never planned on letting him stay. He didn't convince anyone to falsify Roman's Animus test. He made the decision himself then kept Roman's real IN as his ace in the hole.

"Actually, no. This is a biology lesson," I say as I step onto center stage. "It's a good one," I add, mimicking Jakob's Aurora speech. "A woman wants to have sex with a man," I say, pacing about just as he had, "the woman goes to the man ... she runs her hands through his hair ... then down his arms. Slowly, she moves over his hips, coming finally to his inner thighs ... We know how this ends, right? When it comes to sex, biologically speaking, men are at the mercy of women. We are not equal in that regard, are we?"

I study their fearful faces. "Women are more powerful sexually. It's an advantage we have over men, scientifically irrefutable. Plus we can all feel it, can't we? That men are sexually vulnerable to women." They all shift in their seats looking more than a little uncomfortable, but only Jakob's eyes are filled with guilt. He throws his hands in the air.

"Get her out of here," he orders, and one of the black-robed men stands. But the two white-robed men and Marcus Joplin hold him back.

"Leave her," Marcus says, eyeing Jakob. "Go on," he tells me, and for the first time, I realize Jakob has no more authority than the rest of them.

"No one likes to feel vulnerable," I say. "Trust me, Jakob, I get it. But these are the facts. Likewise, men have a certain superior trait over women, biologically speaking. They are stronger ..." I eye Jakob. "Life is really very simple when you break it down, isn't it? It's very basic. You," I point to Jakob, "are stronger than me, by a lot. An awkwardly obvious statement given my appearance, isn't it?"

The other men look at Jakob in shock as he stares me down. "I don't know if you've noticed, but you're also much bigger than me. As a woman, I have a sexual advantage but find myself at a complete physical disadvantage."

I stare unblinking, forcing him to look at me, to look at what he's done, and I see nothing but dread in his eyes. He has no illusions about where I'm heading. He knows. And he can't stop me. I burn him with my stare until his eyes break from mine, then I go on: "I had no chance at all of fending you off ... as you beat and raped me ... repeatedly."

My words hang in the air like raw meat dripping with blood. "That, of course, says absolutely nothing about me, scientifically or otherwise, or any other woman who's ever been raped for that matter. But, if you think about it, raping a woman sure does say a lot about a man. Doesn't it? It says it's *you* who can't be trusted, who mishandles even the most basic power you possess. It says that it's *you* who doesn't know your place," I assess, and see the faces of the other men agreeing with that. "Do you know what Jakob means in

Hebrew?" I ask him of the name my grandfather suggested. "It means, 'he deceives.'" I say. "You are a master of deception for many reasons, but mostly because you aren't a real man. A real man not only accepts a woman's power over him, he reveres her for it."

I walk over to my throne.

"You did a bad thing, Thomas, and karma is real," I finish, standing right beneath my flag, in front of my opulent chair, the seat of a powerless little princess. One I will never sit in.

He knows exactly what I'm going to do next, everyone knows, but no one moves. No one dares. They don't even breathe. And it's a very small task for my skilled hands and trusty ax, decimating a wooden chair, even a grandiose one. I pulverize it in a half-dozen swings.

"The apple from the tree of knowledge strikes again," I say and walk out.

Thomas Greely was the only friend Shamus ever had.

Just before midnight, in Sulfur, as I was dozing off, I startled awake. I'd been trying to fall asleep for more than an hour but every time I began drifting out, the same nightmare kept creeping in.

I was being chased through the desert, through Sulfur. I didn't know by what, not at first, but I was running for my life, bare feet pounding on the cracked tan earth, arms pumping, panting like a wild animal. Finally, I'd turn and see what it was: a dragon, a massive flying reptile monster barreling down, about to incinerate me, getting closer and closer each time I fell back into the dream. I felt the heat of his breath on my neck, then woke again with a violent jerk.

That was when I heard the screeching tires, the blaring horns, and then the impact. It was an earthshattering explosion of smashing glass and crumpling metal, sending shock waves through the RV, the boxy vehicle rocking side to side. I threw the covers off, jumped down from the loft where I slept, and whipped the camper door open so fast the little metal blinds slammed against the glass window as I flew outside.

Only seconds earlier, twenty yards from where I slept, five souls left this earth. One look at the burning wreckage, the overturned eighteen-wheeler inextricably melded into the small station wagon, and anyone could see that this accident was not survivable.

Through the rising smoke, across the road, Shamus stood, slack jawed, his head tilted, his eyes were wide with shock. Cian stood motionless on the other side of the road directly across from Shamus.

Then the truck's engine, having just instantaneously gone from eighty miles per hour to zero, began hissing out a warning. It was at that perilous moment when Shamus rushed in.

After a minute or two, he emerged, bent over, coughing, and dragging a body across the gray pavement toward Cian. It was a man who looked about Shamus's size and age, covered in blood, his head flopped to one side, legs dragging along the asphalt. Shamus retched and gagged from the smoke and maybe from whatever else he saw inside that car, then kneeled down to check the man's vitals. He waved Cian over, but my grandfather just stood watching.

"*Come on!*" Shamus screamed, but Cian didn't move.

Shamus got up off the pavement and ran over to Cian, grabbing him by the arm and pulling him back to the man who appeared to be quite dead. Cian stood over him a minute before kneeling down, hovering his hand over the man's motionless chest another minute before finally pressing into it, palms atop the sternum, tilting his head back, face toward the sky. A blast of wind ripped through the still landscape, sending sand and tumbleweeds tearing down the road, whipping up the sulfuric stench.

I saw the man's leg twitch. I heard a gasp, and his hands came up over his chest. Cian backed away, but Shamus still knelt beside the man, whose head turned to look up at my brother.

The first thing he did was crawl over to the small smashed car. Then, lying on his belly, face smashed into the pavement, he frantically tried to pull the other people out. Shamus stood watching him. I couldn't tell whether he was wiping sweat or tears from his eyes.

After an hour of the man pacing and screaming and vomiting profusely, wailing on the side of the road next to the still smoldering carnage, Shamus listening and working to calm him, the four of us left. The silence was oppressive as the RV floated along the dark road, Shamus at the wheel. Thomas sat on one of the couches in the back, and I sat on the other. He stared off like a zombie, like a man who'd just left his dead wife and two small children trapped inside a mangled car on a remote highway in the middle of the desert. Shamus's eyes flickered up from the road to the rearview mirror every few seconds, checking on Thomas.

We drove to the nearest town—Gerlach, Nevada, population 206.

That's where we left the shell-shocked man, at a rundown Texaco station. I was sent into the convenience store to buy him a bottle of water, which he held limply in his hand. And before we finally left, thankfully heading east and out of the desert, he and Shamus sat on a cement block in front of an empty parking space talking for over an hour.

I had never seen Shamus relate to anyone before that

night. I'd never seen him care about anyone at all. Shamus was more than just a loner. He was more than just "troubled" or "battling demons." He was uninterested in human connections. And on the rare occasion when he did interact with anyone, it was robotic, forced, and uncomfortable for everyone involved.

Kristina was the only other person I ever saw him willingly spend time with, though even a stranger could see that she was much more interested in Shamus than he was in her. She flitted around him like a butterfly as he stood there, letting her, without walking away; that was as close to love as Shamus could get. For whatever mystifying reason, Kristina seemed truly transfixed by him, and being that she was *highly* persistent, he tolerated it. If she were to be hit by a bus, even right in front of him, I don't think he would have cared.

But Shamus was invested in Thomas. *Thomas was different.* So different, looking back, it should have alarmed me. It should have sent bottle rockets shooting out of my brain in all directions. Though for some reason, it didn't. I just accepted it. I never gave it any thought. Once Thomas and Shamus became friends, it was like it had always been that way.

Like it was somehow written in the stars.

SIXTEEN

— ❖ —

I feel resurrected.

Even though my plan has fallen apart and so many things have gone wrong—to say the least—I feel strangely invincible. Maybe it's because it has all fallen apart and everything has gone so terribly wrong ... and I am still here.

I am confident that I've figured out a way to save Val, and that I'll get to Roman in time, and that we'll find a cure. I am even confident that I will fully crack the code, delusional as that conviction is. *All* of it is, to be fair, but it doesn't seem to matter. I am washed in newness; parts of myself have come alive that I've never felt before. There is great stillness inside me. I feel a strange new mix of calm present awareness and raw power. I feel utterly indestructible.

Even before I see Fiorella and Zee.

In combat boots, army fatigues, and with automatic rifles in hand. But they are still a very welcome sight as I waltz out of the great hall, still panting from the throne destruction heard around the world. And when I notice the rifle strapped to Zee's back, I know right away that it's Cian's will. That we're going to Rugby, because Rugby is one of the dots on the map. It's one of the stars of Ophiuchus.

I break into a jog as I near them, and they do the same. Though we haven't spoken once the entire time I've been here, the defiant gleam in Fiorella's eyes tells me everything I need to know.

We run through the halls and passageways, toward where I see Seth, Collins, and Rafe waiting at a door that leads outside to the runway. The door I've watched Roman enter and exit through many times.

"Maricielo's not dead, is he?" I ask through my heavy breathing.

"No, he's not," Fiorella answers. "But Roman thought he was. Everyone thinks he's dead." We burst through the door, ready to storm the helipad, prepared to get to Rugby, no matter what it takes. But the helicopter stands unguarded, fueled, and ready for takeoff. Seth climbs into the driver's seat and stokes the control panel, smiling to himself. "Flew one of these in the Rangers," he says.

The blades begin to turn, and we're soon in the air. I watch out the open window as the sprawling estate of Antiquus grows smaller and smaller in the distance. I'm grateful to be leaving that place and amazed by what they've pulled off. But I was in for an even bigger surprise.

The obedient citizens of Rugby.

Of all the things discovered in their DNA, the spirit of revolt wasn't something I imagined Animus unearthing.

I was wrong.

Rafe tells me about the two thousand or so residents of Rugby who have become a rebel force and who are hell bent on taking down Aurora. It turns out that Rafe and Fiorella have been working closely together, planning this daring escape for some time now. Over the roar of the helicopter, he proudly recounts the weapons they had stolen days ago, the cameras diverted this morning, and all the communication signals that they just jammed.

But it's not until I see it with my own eyes that I believe what they are telling me, that when the unthinkable finally shook humankind all the way to its core and when the rest of the world lost its collective mind, in Rugby they were gathering intelligence, amassing an arsenal, building an army, and lying in wait.

"And I thought they were holding prayer vigils," I say to

Fiorella as I walk with her and Zee through the little town I loved and left behind, now unrecognizable to me. Like it's turned into a military base overnight.

I smile at the sight of Phoenix a block up the road, army fatigues, gun on her hip, waiting to greet us. She hasn't seen her mom, Fiorella, or her sister, Zee, in months. When we reach her, she hugs them both. Though it's easy to see how much she loves them Phoenix is stiff and awkward when it comes to affection.

"Don't they have a gym in Antiquus?" she asks me with a grin.

"It's good to see you too," I tell her. And it is. Just the sight of her, here of all places, exuding strength and independence, it fills me with hope.

Then Phoenix leads us down Main Street toward the town square, where the stone obelisk once stood. In its place I see the highly secured headquarters they've been telling me about, the guards, the watchtowers, and the aerial drones, constantly circling over four steel fortresses.

"Animus Task Force buildings that were commandeered and then transported here from other locations," Phoenix explains. It's the center of an operation I'm struggling to process even exists. How had I not noticed? How had I missed such an elaborate and thorough plan as it unfolded right under my nose?

Phoenix explains how the massive offensive they've waged over the last few months has allowed the resistance to grow well beyond Rugby.

"I'm truly in awe of these people," Fiorella concedes of the residents here. I marvel at them as they pass by, heading here and there; it's apparent they are one unit, one people. It's not in how they look or dress. It's in their eyes. It's the same fearlessness I see in each of them, the same purpose, and the same resolve.

"So this is why they seemed to welcome the Animus test without any real objections, why they so easily submitted to testing, no questions asked ... why they stayed so calm when no one else could ..." I realize, amazed and dumbfounded.

"Exactly," Phoenix says. "And why it wasn't difficult at all for me to break you out that night and steal you away to Antiquus where you needed to be ... *at the time*. We'd just taken control of the whole facility. It had already begun." There's a good deal of Joan of Arc shining through her eyes. "The goons never saw it coming."

I look around in wonder. There is no semblance of the tiny town I left—like the stage props of a play it's all been wheeled away.

"No one's afraid of me anymore," I notice. Even in my bloodied clothes, with my bruised and swollen face, they just go about their business.

"All the people who were afraid of you are the ones who rushed off, who split the second they saw what was happening," Phoenix says. "Afraid to admit that Animus wasn't what they were being told it was. People like that are long gone."

Everything is beginning to make sense. Everything from Cian waking Thomas and how he became Jakob to why I was drawn to Rugby in the first place seems like a flawlessly choreographed series of events.

"This is the epicenter of what has become the movement against Aurora," Fiorella begins to elaborate. It's clear that she feels there's no time to waste. "This tiny population of people, we are the leaders of a vast network of revolutionaries."

"But how did this happen?" I ask. "I mean, how are they able to see Animus for what it is while so many millions of others cannot?"

"Maricielo began working years ago on their awakening, on teaching them to question things, encouraging them to question the world and everything in it," Fiorella says, and my mind snaps to the first thought I had while watching the Animus "sales pitch" in the lobby before my test. When Sourial touted Pheumachronology as the solution to all our problems when she said that it would finally bring about world peace. Because of Maricielo, I knew they weren't telling us how that would work. They weren't really telling us much of anything.

"As soon as we arrived here," Fiorella continues, "Maricielo started engaging people in conversations about life, politics, society, prompting them to question their belief systems, but he had to back off. These days, people are more threatened than ever by independent thinking; they're tightly attached to all the lies the world is telling them."

"When did all this begin?" I wonder.

"The day the Mayan calendar ended," Phoenix says. The very same day Cian woke Thomas. "That was when I first knew what was coming, and I was able to see exactly what we had to do. On December 21, 2012, a great shift occurred. The Earth tilted, the axis of the sun wobbling away from its alignment with Orion to align with Ophiuchus instead. We moved from The Gate of Man to The Gate of the Gods; now we're able to pass into the fifth dimension and begin the sixth epoch."

"Are you kidding me?" I ask. "I've spent the last month struggling to string all of that together. When are you going to start telling me all these things ahead of time? Why don't you just tell me how it all ends? Tell me what happens next."

"Because I don't know," Phoenix admits, and Fiorella

nods. "I don't know how we get from here to there. I know something else has to happen, but I don't know *what*. It's all stopped, the knowing. Over the last month it just … it slowly drifted away."

"The same thing has happened to Roman," I say, and concern darkens Phoenix and her mother's faces.

"I would've sworn you weren't coming back. I was certain of it, actually," Phoenix says.

I think of how I almost didn't, how I was getting sucked into the illusion, seduced by the promise of power Maricielo warned about.

As Phoenix studies me, I know her well enough to know that she's trying to locate my true intentions, to pinpoint my allegiance. What's in my heart? Am I here on behalf of Aurora, or am I here to help destroy it? When she places an automatic rifle in my hand, I gather she's figured it out.

"It's good to have you back," she says, then smirks. "You always did love this podunk town."

"Rugby, North Dakota," I say. "Best place in the whole damn world."

It's buzzing inside the headquarters. Like command central for a shuttle launch, people walking purposefully from here to there, endless rows of computer terminals, an air of high stakes and tense determination, and an imposing screen at the front of it all.

Maricielo comes striding toward me, flanked by Val's husband, Porter.

I find out very quickly that Val is still alive, and that they already know what Jakob did to Roman. I even get an update on how he's doing.

"He hasn't developed any symptoms yet," Porter says to my relief.

Here in Rugby, they've been intercepting the video feeds from both Primitus and Antiquus—*all of them*. They don't just know about the statuses of Val and Roman, they know everything.

"Every detail is important," Maricielo explains.

Like the fact that they know Jude is still very much in love with me. And that they're unsure of how he's going to react to my new relationship with Roman when he finds out. Which he hasn't yet.

When I point out that it's not a *new* relationship, technically, I'm told that is completely irrelevant.

"Jude holds Primitus stable," Porter says. "He's the only thing that holds it stable, the only calming force. And his state of mind matters a great deal."

Maricielo swipes a monitor, pulling an interactive map onto the screen displaying both Antiquus and Primitus and all of North America with other spots lit up.

"In addition to Rugby, there are eleven strongholds," Porter says. "Places like Fairbanks, Juneau, Vancouver, Alberta, Winnipeg, Seattle, Nashville, Albuquerque—they're all anti-Aurora safe havens.

"Ophiuchus," I say, turning the image ninety degrees. The points on the map, including the strongholds, Rugby, Antiquus and Primitus, all line up perfectly with the stars of the constellation—a coincidence that, by now, doesn't even surprise me.

A gleam in his eye, Maricielo grins. "Have I told you yet how good it is to have you back, Eve?" he asks.

"It's good to be back."

Shaking his head and marveling at the map, "Just one more sign that we're standing on the right side of history."

Then Gaebe walks up and clears his throat.

I'm sure he can tell that I'm confused at the sight of him and thinking of our last encounter. As I was locked up in a cell, he told me that he was "just holding the key so it didn't fall into the wrong hands," the key I watched Jude give him. The one I believe unlocks Cian's nightstand.

"Jude didn't want to go with Shamus; he *had* to go with Shamus," Phoenix says as Gaebe takes the key from around his neck and hands it to me.

"For you," he says. "It's yours. You were right. I was holding it for you until you got back. And of course, you're also right about what it opens."

Cian's nightstand. But how would Jude have had the key to a piece of furniture that had been in my grandfather's possession since …

"Jude's father … James," I whisper, stunned by how it all makes sense. "Our trip to Alaska."

"Jude's father is a carpenter," Phoenix says. "He built it for Cian, who then locked it, after presumably placing something inside, and gave the key to Jude, who has worn it around his neck since that very day when he was five years old."

I slip the key around my own neck. I can't help thinking of the connection it holds between Jude and me. About my constant fascination with seeing what was inside the nightstand while the key was around Jude's neck as I dreamed of him constantly. And all of this long before we ever met. And since my fate is to unlock the code that will send humanity into the fifth dimension, Jude must be a part of that puzzle. He might even know something about the code I'm searching for.

"So Jude isn't—I mean, he's …" I stammer, thinking of my latest haunting dream and how he seems completely like himself in it, the person he was before he went to Primitus.

"He's playing both sides," Maricielo says, "just as they

did." He puts his arm around Fiorella and nods to Zee. I'm relieved to know that with Val and now Roman both in Primitus, Jude is there, and that he's looking out for them.

"Jude is our eyes and our ears, and he's also doing in Primitus what I did here in Rugby," Maricielo says. "He's awakening them, only he's accomplished in three months what took me the better part of ten years."

"Classic Jude," Phoenix quips. "Always with his hair on fire."

I see Jude's face on the large screen and walk toward it. "What's he doing?" I ask.

Phoenix steps next to me as I watch what looks to be a live feed from Primitus. Jude strums a guitar surrounded by swooning women, all barely dressed, with flowers in their hair, twirling and dancing like hippies. They look high as can be—whether it's on life or drugs is hard to tell.

"He's doing what he does," Maricielo remarks.

"Shamus had planned to use Jude as a sort of idol, to be a distraction," Phoenix says. "A diversion from the totalitarian rule. When Jude got to Primitus, he was taught to sing. And to play the guitar. Of course he exceled at it, going on to quickly master not just the guitar but the piano, drums, you name it. And he doesn't just sing," she shakes her head, "he transports people." Raising her eyebrows as if to warn me, "Turn it up please," she asks a woman sitting at a computer nearby. "Shamus planned to use him to galvanize the masses into a sort of religion, a cult of new souls."

When I hear the first notes, it's hard to process that the music is coming from a person I know. But it's not hard to imagine why Shamus thought Jude could inspire a religious cult. I'm breathless.

"I told you," Phoenix says. "He's transfixing."

"You should hear him sing 'Stairway to Heaven,'" Porter quips. "It's like an acid trip—so I've heard."

"It's like he's been doing this his whole life," Gaebe remarks as Jude serenades the hordes of people.

"It's unexplainable really." Maricielo shakes his head. "The amazing thing was watching him go from never singing or playing a note to this in a matter of days. He makes a song by the damn Beatles somehow sound like it was written for him, for the express purpose of him singing it in this moment."

He's right. Jude's rendition of "Imagine" is unlike anything I've ever heard—real, raw, and incredibly moving. In Primitus, they sway and twirl under the desert moonlight, and here in Rugby we stare with mouths agape.

"Mute it, please," Phoenix asks the woman, who takes away the sound. "We literally have to keep it on silent or we'll all just stand there in a trance. The whole thing wasn't quite going the way Shamus thought it would. The people not only worship Jude, but they also listen to him, and Shamus is getting very frustrated, and frustrated by Jude, the way he just … speaks the truth."

"If there's one thing Shamus hates," I add.

"Exactly, the truth is not going to do. And Jude just can't stick to the script Shamus wants. He can't tell people that they belong in these groups. Jude doesn't believe in Animus, and he refuses to lie. Shamus hadn't anticipated that at all. So he sort of cast him out, downgraded him from life with the elite King souls to the outskirts. But he continues enlightening more and more people. Shamus even tried drugging him."

"Scopolamine?" I ask.

"Yup, same thing they use in Antiquus, but in Antiquus they have Jakob there to control the message and an infrastructure to administer the drug. In Primitus, things are … well, not so orderly. We also believe the drug has no effect of Jude. He seems to be evolving rapidly. We know he can see in the dark, perfectly in the pitch dark, and he no longer sleeps at all."

"Wait—he's *evolving*?" I ask.

"It's just a guess," Maricielo says. "This is uncharted territory for all of us, but it seems he's got one foot in the fifth dimension and one here."

"You're not worried Shamus is just going to have him killed?" I ask.

"No," Maricielo answers right away.

"Why not? I'd think that would be his next move."

"Shamus knows the whole place will collapse into revolt," Phoenix says.

"Seriously?" I ask. "*Collapse?*"

Phoenix shakes her head. "You have no idea."

Though he may not be able to kill Jude like he surely wants to, Shamus is big on shooting things out of the sky. His kingdom may be wildly unsecured on the ground, but it's outfitted with a state-of-the-art PAC-3 radar and Stunner-based PAAC-4 surface-to-air missiles salvaged from the United States military. Killing things that would dare to fly anywhere near Primitus has apparently been Shamus's favorite pastime.

That's why Phoenix and I will have to drive to Primitus.

We're leaving at dawn, and our plan is ironclad. We know the precise locations of both Val and Roman. There are people on the ground in Primitus to help us, people like Draya and Payge who are also playing both sides. And members of the Aion Dorea who, like Clio, Bronwyn, and Pythagoras, can't give me any answers but can offer us protection. I'm confident we will get in and get out. But my thoughts make it hard to fall asleep.

Knowing that I still have to crack the code and that time is ticking and that we can't take Jude with us without destabilizing the entire place is bothering me. Something about it just doesn't feel right.

Staring up at the ceiling at the battle of the fallen angels painted above the bed where I sleep in Phoenix's house, my thoughts turn to the last time I lay here. It was with Jude. And I remember all the feelings I had that night, of desire, of wanting to kiss him, and of concern as he wrestled with the nagging idea of why he had always felt so different. All of it only further confusing my already restless mind.

Before I headed to bed, as Maricielo and I cleaned up after the dinner he and Fiorella made for the thirty people who ate around their enormous kitchen table, I told him about the dream I've been having. About the ice and Jude and my own death. He just listened as I spoke, just as Cian would have, then he asked a few questions, most of which were about the caribou.

"He is your spirit animal," he finally concluded.

"What do you mean?" I asked.

"A spirit animal is a presence, an energy that shows up when your soul is pulling it toward your consciousness. So it's your soul that's showing you the caribou. And what that spirit animal represents is your message. The meaning of the caribou is a transition through darkness, discovering that which is hidden, and a deep connection to your true home over very long distances."

Then he kissed the top of my head and went off to bed. "Tomorrow's a big day, try and get some rest."

I'm certain he meant for his words to be reassuring, though for some reason I found his assessment unsettling, even disturbing. And I had no doubt at all that he was correct. Especially the part about 'my true home,' which, as Clio said, is not Earth.

SEVENTEEN

— ❖ —

The law of opposites, that's all I can think of as Phoenix and I slink through the darkness. Unlike the stringent order in Antiquus, the heavy surveillance and Big Brother stare, Primitus is a whole different kind of disastrous creation.

The chaos is obvious and apparent—and incredibly alarming, even from a hundred yards out. Along one side of the immense circus-like spectacle, thick smoke billows off into the warm desert air from a raging fire, and it doesn't appear that any attempts are being made to put it out. We see figures and shadows running about and hear the guttural sounds of human distress.

Just on the other side of the complex, laser lights in every imaginable color dance in rhythmic circles in the sky. Enormous white triangles of fabric, like the sails of a ship, billow gracefully in the whipping wind above opulent sand-colored structures, and the pounding beat of techno music pumps endlessly. It's unlikely the screams from one side are even being heard on the other. Though in Antiquus, the sense of who we are is a complete fabrication, one look at Primitus and anyone can see that there is no community here at all. That chaos will work in our favor.

There are multiple large gaps in the crumbly concrete wall that marks the border, and entering is jarringly easy. And though I have no doubt that Shamus is attempting to draw us in, I'm certain it's not his brilliant masterminding but the lawlessness, disorder, and lack of leadership that make this desert city so incredibly simple to invade.

The only other thing we have to do tonight is meet up with Kali. She's a member of the Aion Dorea who, like Bronwyn, Clio, and Pythagoras believes the awakening can no longer be held back. She's expecting us to arrive shortly in what's become of the Warrior sector.

Draya and Payge meet us as planned at a designated fracture in the wall, which Phoenix has termed G-22.

Draya and Payge's Animus tests determined them to be Guardian souls. Upon their arrival here, they were issued long white dresses, white headscarves, and brown clogs. Guardians are seen as the caretakers, nurses, and general helpers of the masses—and here in Primitus that's been a very big job, which is evident the second I see them. After nearly four months here, what's left of their torn and tattered dresses reveals deeply browned and burned skin over their stomachs, backs, and legs. The soles of their clogs are held to their feet by strings wrapped up their legs, and the white headscarves are now tied around their waists like sarongs, splattered with the blood of all those they have tried to help.

"It's just one lavish ongoing party," Draya tells us of the hordes of people crawling like ants around a space-age sand castle in the center of a swanky beach, minus the ocean. The optimism and the light in her eyes are gone. From her terse words and stoic manner, her goal is obvious: blot out the force that orphaned her and move on.

"The Gypsy sector used to extend all the way out here," Payge says. "They used to occupy the largest outer ring around the city, spread comfortably in a sort of lavish hippie commune. The first few days in each sector were like a paradise on Earth, but after just a few weeks, everything changed dramatically. For the Gypsies, the violence and the rapes began to drive them from this far side and from the other directly across from it. Now they congregate in a smaller area on the western outskirts."

"It's been a bloody and terrifying process," Draya says. She tells how the massive circle of people organized in rings—Kings in the center, Guardians encircling them, then Warriors. and then finally Gypsies—has morphed into a straight line in a matter of months.

"The dead are transported out daily. And some of whom are near death," she says, her low solemn voice racked with both grief for the loss of her parents and disgust. It's just as Roman had thought: Primitus is dumping not only the dead but also some who are still living. And they were all from within these walls.

Back in Rugby, Porter had shown me a time-lapsed video of aerial images that revealed a bizarre phenomenon. First the Kings spread out in a long swath from the already enormous epicenter they occupied, all the way to the eastern wall. That's what really set off the chaos. And in a matter of just one week, the shape of where people lived in this walled-off city went from a flower to a snake.

"It's the resources," Phoenix adds. "They're tightly controlled. People began to congregate for survival."

We pass one tent like structure after the next. All of them are tattered and dilapidated. I pull back a torn drape and look inside one every now and again. At first, they are always empty. But as we make our way from the back wall toward the center and begin to near the Warrior sector, each tent contains a different scene.

In one there may be a few people sleeping, passed out, or dead, lying on one another in clumps. And in the next, there may be a crime in progress, someone being assaulted, beaten, or raped. Either way, we have to walk on. We can't draw any attention to ourselves. We just have to keep going.

Eventually I stop looking.

As we move into the Warrior sector, where the fire rages a hundred yards ahead, we begin to wind through dizzying rings of concentric streets that are paved in packed dirt and lined with tiny shacks like doublewide doghouses. It feels like we're rats in a maze.

"Stay closer now," Phoenix says, and we move into a tighter pack. The cracking of the fire and the howls of those nearby it are growing louder. The streets become more and more crowded the closer we get to the blaze.

"Where is she?" I ask as we pass by the hundredth shelter, thinking that in each one we come upon we'll find the mysterious Kali holed up inside, our Aion Dorea guide, where I imagine she'll be studying maps of the night sky.

"It's not much further," Payge assures me.

Draya just raises her eyebrows to Payge.

"What?" I ask.

"We have to go all the way to the edge of the fire," Phoenix says.

And that's exactly what we do.

If Phoenix lives a few thousand more Warrior lifetimes, spends a couple of centuries fighting orcs in an underworld, takes a lethal amount of steroids, and grows even taller, she may be like Kali one day.

Taunting the fire like a dragon sorceress, arms extended into the air and cackling at the sky, we find Kali at the center of a tribe of Warriors dancing around the roaring blaze.

Kali tells us she's the source of the fire.

"And when this one burns out, we'll start another," her voice commands the attention of anyone nearby. "Burning our way to the center."

"We are always on the march," she declares, which would explain the poles and tattered drapes that combine to make their transient shelter where we will be staying the night.

If Bronwyn is my spirit mother, Kali is Phoenix's.

As we sit inside a mobile bastion of weaponry surrounded by heavily muscled guards, Phoenix and Kali are already dynamically in sync and preparing the battle plan that will take place over the course of a single night—tomorrow. I sit on the ground, drawing circles in the dusty sand, half listening.

"Eve, what are you doing?" asks Kali's booming voice.

"Sorry," I say, brushing the sand from my hands.

"Maybe I'm just thirsty. I'm having a hard time staying focused."

"What I mean is, why are you even sitting here?" Her intense glare seems to penetrate into my heart. "You want to go find Jude—go find him. You think he's got answers for you, and yet you sit here drawing circles in the sand." She stares at me for a moment then goes back to her conversation without missing a beat.

Before I leave, Kali insists that I'll get all the way out to the eastern wall on my own. She believes my abilities are "limitless, to be honest," that I can do things even she can't, like walk through fire, bend matter with my mind, and fly. And though I think that all sounds really fun, I decide to take several guards with me on the off chance none of that works out.

I've also decided that she's stark raving mad.

A huge fan of Jude's, Payge asks if she could tag along. And we are like two tiny peanuts in a shell of guards as we wind eastward through the other side of the Warrior sector, where the circular streets give way to a wide-open expanse.

"I never got to thank you for what you did for me in Rugby with my test," I say, marveling at our matching eyes and that I'm standing with the soul of the little girl I lost centuries ago, Lucia.

"You mean what I *tried* to do for you," Payge says,

clearly disappointed that her efforts were thwarted.

"By the way, why did you decide to help me?"

"I don't know, really. When I saw your number, I was afraid of what would happen to you."

I smile at her, this sweet girl around my own age who seems a hundred years younger. "Once, in a past life, you were my daughter."

Her eyes fix on me, glowing with curiosity.

"It was a traumatic lifetime, one where we both learned a great deal. Lessons we carry with us still. Fight or flight, split-second decisions, the deep love of family," I say, feeling tremendous gratitude to have her here with me again.

Like fairies flitting through the night, several Gypsies twirl by. Their heads whirling, their eyes closed, music in their minds only they can hear.

"Are they on some kind of drug?" I ask one of the guards. She doesn't answer or even acknowledge my question.

"Peyote," says the guard walking directly in front of us without turning around. We pass two people down on all fours howling at the moon. They appear to be fully convinced they are coyotes.

"Have you tried it?" I ask Payge, who shakes her head fearfully.

"No way."

Just beyond them, I spot a large canopy where twenty tents have been strung together. It's dimly lit by the glow of just a few candles. I hear the calming strum of an old Jim Croce song, "Time in a Bottle," and I know that this is where I'll find Jude.

"Brother Jude" is what they insist we call him. We're instructed to remove our shoes before stepping into the tent. We also have to whirl around, expelling evil spirits until we're too dizzy to stand and stagger to the ground.

"That's when we know they're all gone," a tall and thin crazy-eyed man explains from the inside of the tent. He holds up a withered arm, not yet permitting us to pass.

"Eve," Jude's voice calls out. "Let her in."

I raise my eyebrows, grab Payge's arm, and walk past the man straight to Jude, who, like a modern-day maharaja, is sitting atop a mound of pillows and surrounded by mostly naked and leggy teenage women. His smile is a ray of sunlight, his eyes shining like diamonds reflecting firelight.

It's funny to watch how star struck Payge is at the sight of him.

"Hello, Brother Jude." I fold my hands in prayer position and bow.

He shakes his head. "I keep telling them not to call me that."

"What in the hell is all this about?" I ask. "And what's going on with your eyes?" It's so dim inside the tent, the few candles scattered about, lifting the space to only a couple of shades above total dark. And yet Jude's eyes are starkly visible, as if they're being backlit from inside his head.

He doesn't answer either question. He just looks at me, a bit like Kali, observing me intensely.

"Do you want to do peyote, Eve?" he asks with a little smirk. It's typical of him to be random and abrupt, taking his cues from someplace else, from strange forces the rest of us don't see or hear, but still, his question catches me by surprise.

I look at Payge, whose eyes are wide with fear. "I have thought about it," I admit after a few seconds. Twice it has crossed my mind, to be exact. Once when I was in Vana, the holy forest, when I learned that's where things like peyote and ayahuasca come from, that natural psychedelics were a gift to humanity from beyond to expand our minds and for reminding us of our connection to the divine source of all life. And one other time, when I first watched the video of Jude singing and wondered if the Gypsies I saw had taken it.

A girl in a long skirt and a ratty strapless bra wanders by and places a little dried-up cactus button in my hand, a peyote fairy of sorts.

"You just eat it," she whispers, exuding seduction.

"Thanks," I say as she floats off. For a second, I stare at the withered little ball in my palm, then I put it in my pocket and sit down next to Jude, thinking of all the things I want to say to him and all the things I don't, thinking of the code I've got to break, and how, if anyone, has access to forbidden secret knowledge it's Jude. And also thinking of how much I love Roman, how deeply and madly I've fallen for him.

"We've got to talk," I say.

EIGHTEEN

—— ✠ ——

Maybe it's because all four of us are in one place.

That's my first thought when, just seconds after I sit down next to Jude, a billion locusts seem to ascend into the world from the center of the earth all at once. Maybe we *are* the four beings from the four corners of the earth and this *is* the tribulation I've been accused of setting off. The thought races through my mind as Jude and I jump up. I grab Payge's arm and we take off running.

It's hard to see any other reason for the eruption of madness brought by ravenous swarms of jet-black winged grasshoppers that dive-bomb through every inch of the air around us. It's hard to see anything at all. The serene tent where I was pretty sure that an orgy was about to begin has exploded into insanity.

"Come on," Jude yells, grabbing my hand and pulling

me forward as I drag Payge behind me. We dash from the tent and tear toward the wall encircling the city, which is about two hundred feet away. I hear screams and turn around to see a handful of people covered in fire tearing through the thick insect cloud toward the abandoned Gypsy tents. "Oh my god," I breathe out as a man collapses into a tent, igniting it, a fire that spreads to several others as his screams join the roar of the locusts.

I pull on Payge's arm, but she's frozen in place. Paralyzed by terror, shaking her head at me, a far-off look in her eyes.

"Eve, come on!" Jude shouts. "She can't move. Leave her, she'll be okay."

Trusting him, I take off and run with Jude to a gap in the partially collapsed wall. We slip out into the desert, where there isn't a single locust.

"What is happening?" I yell, barely able to make myself heard over the horrifying screams of desperate humanity on the other side of the wall and the ceaseless howls of the wind.

"They don't know," is all he says, shaking his head, his otherworldly eyes glowing neon in the dark.

"They don't know what?"

"It's only in there, each time this happens, I tell them. I say next time run outside the walls." He stares off as he talks, utterly amazed by what he's explaining, "Anyone can leave, I say to them. You can go at any time, I tell them over and over. None of this is real. None of this is real. None of this is real."

"But ... where are the locusts coming from?" I ask. "How often does this happen?"

"They're bringing them in with their thoughts, from—"

"From Abasus," I say. He nods, his glowing eyes fixed on me.

Abasus, the place I never wanted to think of ever again.

At some point during my six weeks of grief and insanity, I slipped into a bottomless place. I instantly knew I'd been there before—just not during an actual lifetime—and that it was called Abasus, that it was the sixth of seven underworlds, where no suffering was withheld. It was a black hole of everlasting torment.

Abasus was a rift, a ravine where there was nothing to grab onto, where all you could do was fall deeper and deeper, and the deeper you fell, the darker it got, and the darker the thinner the atmosphere and the faster you plummeted into the ever-expanding darkness. It was propelled entirely by the cumulative energy of human fear. Worst of all, it was filled with maddening screams that never ceased.

The second I realized I wasn't getting out of Abasus

through death—a strange door appeared beside me as I continued to fall. A colossal marble door intricately carved from top to bottom with hundreds of men, some climbing upward, some clinging on wherever they could, some falling. One man near the top sat alone—he appeared to be thinking—and three who were larger than the rest stood at the top, calmly above all the others.

I continued my terrifying descent, watching the door as it followed beside me. When I finally decided to approach it, I felt my soul peel away from my body like two pieces of tape that had been stuck together, and though I saw my body continue to fall when I looked behind me, I was standing firmly on the doorstep. There was no knob or handle of any kind. I pushed on the marble, and it swung open with ease. Peering inside, I couldn't see anything. As far as I could tell it led nowhere, into nothing, but I wondered if at least my soul could rest there so I walked in. Finding some relief, gradually, I stepped farther and farther inside, careful to leave the door open behind me at first. But the unending cries of human suffering drove me to push it closed, and when I did, a scroll appeared before me.

Written on top were the words "The Time Has Come To Choose." In the middle of the long parchment was the word "Fear," and next to it the words "No Fear."

Then there was a pen in my hand. I had to choose. But

I began to understand that it wasn't as simple of a choice as it seemed. One might instantly react and say "No Fear," of course, taking the option of fear off the table, forever… still, it got even more complicated than that.

If I chose "Fear," I would have to forfeit my life as Eve. I would have to leave that body behind, not through death of that body but through me—the soul inside the body—abandoning ship, so to speak. Leaving Evelyn in a soulless animated state to roam the earth as the embodiment of fear disguised as a human and spreading it everywhere she went.

If I chose "No Fear," I would have to go back through the door and leap into the torturous unknown.

"I know that place … there's something there I left undone," I say to Jude, who by the look on his face fully understands. "I choose *not* to make a choice."

"Why?" he asks, plain and curious, reminding me of the night on the cliff, when he asked me why he shouldn't linger dangerously near the edge.

"I just didn't," I say. "Somehow I detached instead."

It was when I detached that what I call "the exorcism stage" began. I was flailing and possessed, occupied, quite literally, by demons. Because I left without choosing, my detachment created a vacuum. As soon as the space opened up, they zoomed in. I hid in the darkest corner I could find from the girl who looked vaguely like me as she thrashed on the bed, her wild eyes zeroing in on mine every now and again. Threatening to go devour my soul where I'd left it, taunting me, knowing I knew how easily it could be done. That she knew where it had gone better than I did.

When the grip of those hungry ghosts finally subsided, I entered the next stage, "the zombie stage," after the demons departed, leaving me an empty vessel until the entire universe seemed to contract to instantly rejoin me with my body.

Then came "the catatonic stage." I was finally present again, but from behind an unblinking and empty stare. I was lost in the cavernous remains of who I was, nothing where I'd left it; almost everything inside me had been rearranged, torn down, or excavated. The rest was charred ruins.

"Your problem wasn't the choice; it was your *perception* of the choice," Jude says. "Perception is everything in this world. Perception and power, they're the building blocks of this entire reality."

"What did you say?" I ask, but he doesn't answer.

"Don't be afraid." He starts to center himself, closing his eyes and breathing slowly. Even though I know we're going back to Abasus, I am remarkably calm. And in a blink we are there.

There is no falling, and there are no screams. We enter silently and slowly walk through the black space, our steps echoing through the vast nothingness. Everything I'd experienced in Abasus is gone. Now it's hollow and still, like the whole thing was only ever a soundstage of sorts.

It's only a blank canvas ... on which perceived fears could be cast, I think into Jude's mind.

Not even the scroll you perceived was really there, he responds as he turns toward me with a large glass jar in his hands. I watch it flicker in and out of sight like it's made of lightning. It's also only perceived, I realize, and knowing instantly what he wants me to do, I grab on to it. Both of our hands hold it steady as a billion locusts get sucked through it, a black river of insects flash flooding toward the jar and into nothingness, like they're sucked through a black hole.

When it's over, there isn't anything in our hands. No jar. He only perceived it there so I could understand what we were doing. But we didn't need it. And then I also understand, instantly, that Jude has been doing this at least once every day.

It's time for this illusion to come to an end, I hear his words in my heart. *Power and perception have run their course.*

And we're standing in the desert again, as if we never left.

Jude and I walk through the devastation toward the Warrior sector. The people who aren't burned to death are stumbling around dazed or crying out in anguish, shaking with fear, and as Jude points out, "Already imagining the swarm's return."

We enter Kali's tent, where she and Phoenix are relatively calm and collected, though Phoenix appears mystified.

"We ran outside the walls where there were no bugs or fire at all, but no one else would follow us," she says. "I tried to lead them, I shouted, some of them I even grabbed, but they preferred to run head on into the fire. The harder I tried, the more of them went sprinting to their deaths."

Then, seeming to snap from one side of her brain to the other, Phoenix whirls around. "Why couldn't we see any of this happening? Why didn't we see the locusts on any of the surveillance videos?"

"The locusts aren't really ..." Kali says, her words failing her. I can tell what she's thinking. Perhaps by the look in her eyes. Or perhaps I can hear it telekinetically: *It's very difficult to explain these kinds of things when our souls are so heavy inside our bodies, and we're walking around on Earth.*

His clear blue eyes shining like beacons in the night, Jude nods slightly, though I don't think she meant to send us her thoughts or even knows we've both collected them somehow.

"Do you want to explain?" Jude asks me.

I close my eyes and take a deep breath. "Fear is a physically contagious energy. It's a vibration that is passed like a bad cold from one to another, disrupting and altering the vibration of the next person, changing it, tuning it, and when enough of them sync up ..."

"They perceive horrors into their immediate reality," Jude continues. "If you don't perceive them, you won't see them. They won't exist for you."

Phoenix looks stunned. "Why is this happening," she asks. "Why are they 'creating this'?"

"It started when I began to explain that Animus wasn't stopping anything," Jude says. "Their natural tendency was to assume that meant bad things would keep coming, that it was all up to some other force out of their control. Even though I told them the truth, that Shamus caused the events and the unthinkable and that he'd been cut off after that, unable to access any realms other than this one, just like you and Roman. But still, people would lay awake at night dreaming of what would come next. They began talking about it. I watched as they all decided it would be locusts. That that's what would come next. Then they manifested the locusts."

After that there is nothing more to say. Phoenix is obviously exhausted, having driven for twenty-four hours straight and then arriving to be besieged by locusts and overloaded with things that are extremely hard to understand. Kali paces vigilantly around the tent, seeming to grow more and more uneasy as the night wears on.

Jude and I lie on our backs looking up at the stars.

I'm not remotely tired. In fact, it feels like I will never sleep again. And I don't want to miss the darkness. I can feel it charging me, opening something inside my head like a door to another dimension.

I examine my hand. Looking at what Jakob had done to me, at the purple-black imprints of hands bruised into my wrists. I don't feel sadness; I'm not even sorry it had happened. I feel no attachment to the event whatsoever. I tell my cells to heal the bruises more quickly, and then I watch as my skin returns to normal before my eyes.

"Jude?" I ask, just as I realize what is happening. It's the same thing that Maricielo speculated had happened to Jude. I am moving into the fifth dimension. My pineal gland is opening up, the portal through which the Mayans and all those who came before them entered into this higher dimension. I have one foot here and one foot there—a there that is still "here," but a completely different version of this world. One where stars don't shine, they *grow* toward you, where you can see the fire that has burned out wafting through space in real time.

"Yes," he says, answering my question. That he can also see into space, just like I can. Our eyes are more powerful than any telescope that has ever existed. And the sky is a feast for us to behold, a bounty of whirling planets and swaths of stardust. When you can see gravity and mass and magnetism and feel everything you see coursing through you at the same time ... the whole world is love and magic.

At the thought of love, Roman dances into my mind, and I feel my heart explode. The immense love I feel for him somehow expands to even more, filling the whole world like a mushroom cloud.

And Maricielo was right. Jude loves me too. He loves me with the reverence of a billion suns. And I feel every bit of it as he lies there next to me. I can feel his heart beating my name. And I love him. But if I don't love him, he won't be hurt; he won't be bothered at all. That's where Maricielo is wrong. That is third-dimensional love. If I don't love Jude, he will understand with his whole heart and with every part of his consciousness what it means: that I haven't arrived yet into the fifth dimension. It's not possible to take anything personally in the fifth dimension. There is no jealousy and there are no feelings to hurt. Feelings that can be hurt are all ego based. They require an elaborate construct of individuality and a sense of identity just to exist. Feelings that can be hurt aren't part of the experience in etheric places like this. All that exists here is unconditional love.

I turn my eyes from the sky to Jude, and he does the same. We look into one another from a perspective unlike any other that exists on Earth. I watch the language that was spoken to me in Kosmos by the serpent mother pour into and out of the top of Jude's head, like a stream of music you can see. Glowing singsong notes that are an ancient language, the Lemarian language of light. He seems to be watching the same thing on me.

Ancient words course through my veins: *Separateness, in all forms, is a fear-based, human-created illusion. All identity is a fantasy, a trick of the mind. When falsely agreed upon by humanity, separateness becomes an elaborate fairy tale. There is no good and evil because there is no separateness.*

It was just as I'd seen in Einstein's theory: there is no good and evil.

Then, compelled by the divine language, I look at my hand. The M glows iridescent, shimmering and radiant in the center of my palm, just like in my dream. As my eyes dissolve into it, the sharp angles begin to round. As it curves into a softer m shape, I finally understand the full meaning and why it's been appearing to me—because it's the thirteenth letter of the Kabbalistic Hebrew alphabet, the "Mem." It symbolizes the womb, and creation, represents water and means, "end, final, limitless." Revealed by the divine mother I met in Kosmos, it's always been there like a lifeline between us, so that I may hear and translate the truth from her to the world: that the nine soul types have been created by man as another new way to divide and control the masses by locking them into the illusion of identity, of separate perspectives. Some will not be able to see it and some will. Her sacred knowledge *is* The Tree of Life. And with it I will set them free: from the Gate of Man to The Gate of The Gods, from Orion to Ophiuchus, from illusion to truth.

Glancing over at Jude, he's doing the very same thing, staring up at the glowing letter on his hand. We put them together, one shinning M coming to rest on top of the other, tightly intertwining our fingers. We hold each other's hand and gaze back out at the galaxy.

I feel radiance like a radioactive frequency coming through our hands. It travels up and down my whole being like I am a highway of divinity, paving me with light, supercharging me with love for all things, all creatures, all life, all people, all of us woven from one fabric, indivisible.

We both feel what the other is feeling because we are one. We feel love and appreciation for everything in existence, everything. We understand everything there is to understand, including the formless consciousness that we are.

We understand that we can even make love right now if we choose to do that, and it would be beautiful and sacred and divine, pouring all of this miraculous love into one another.

But we decide just to watch the stars instead. Drawing Earth's energy up through our backs, into our bodies, holding all life within our intertwined hands, our souls shining out through our eyes, time traveling to all galaxies on a wave of love.

NINETEEN

———— ❈ ————

When morning comes, I realize something very important.

I realize that it's contrast that defines things. The more subtle the contrast the less definition, the starker the contrast the more definition you will perceive. And there is nothing subtle or gradual about the sunrise in the desert. There is a great deal of contrast as the sky goes from full dark to a midday blaze in little more than a five-minute span.

And I don't like the sun for some reason—not any more.

"Melatonin activates the pineal gland," Jude explains as the blessed darkness rapidly gives way to blistering yellow light, and he feels me slipping back from the ethereal place I'd gotten to. I feel like an angel falling from the sky, collapsing into the dusty earth in a heap of busted wings, flying feathers, and anger.

"That's how it is," he says when I sit up and scurry back into the shade of Kali's tent. His voice is tender and understanding, but it doesn't help much. My gut is twisted with something wretched—*hunger*—and my head is pounding from dehydration, and I'm agitated to have to care for a body I'm suddenly not sure that I even need at all.

"I didn't take that peyote last night, did I?" I ask like a disoriented junkie coming down from an epic bender. Jude laughs.

"No," he says. "You just got a little glimpse of life in the fifth dimension."

"A little glimpse?" I ask, stunned.

He nods, emphatic. "The transition is never fun."

"Does it ever get better?" I ask of the horridness I'm experiencing. It's like having to relive being born, right now, at this age: jarring, beyond awkward, and remarkably uncomfortable.

"It will. When we don't have to go back and forth anymore," he says, reminding me of the task at hand: awakening, enlightenment. Taking all of humanity to the place, the one where we belong. But it's so hard to stay focused with the sun searing into my eyes.

To make matters worse, I have to pee.

"I assume I just squat anywhere?" I shout over to where

Kali is doing tai chi, hearing myself sound like a spoiled brat, a snob from some other better planet, and deciding I need to get a handle on this dimensional shift thing before it seriously gets the better of me.

"Over there." She points to a few abandoned tents, their ripped fabric billowing in the hot breeze. I walk off to go squat behind one, shielding my eyes from the revolting sun and relentless sheets of blowing sand and grumbling to myself about how I much prefer glowing radiant highways of source love, how I prefer angel wings and nebulae and stardust to peeing behind a shabby desert tent—like I'm complaining about the service and amenities of a hotel.

As I drop my jeans to my ankles and try my best not to urinate on them and myself, I catch it again: the irrational and yet somehow overwhelming feeling of irritation at having to be stuck in a human body.

"Eve, focus," I tell myself. "You have a job to—" Suddenly, a hand covers my mouth and another one sweeps me up from the ground in one silent swoop.

There are three things I want to perceive out of my own reality. But hard as I try, I can't seem to. Kazaar, Bael, and Druscilla. The Aion Dorea's Primitus counterparts of Sourial, Rasuil, and Ansel, who all want to stay the current course. Who all believe their job remains to keep humanity asleep.

They're dressed in opulence, the two brutish men and one curvy woman, all dripping with jewels, donning designer haute couture, like they're walking down Rodeo Drive instead of through the barren desert, playing the part of King souls like they're gunning for an Academy Award. I'm certain this is crossing the line. As far as the serpent woman I encountered in Kosmos is concerned they can't help. Though I may have assumed that meant they also cannot hinder—which I'm quickly realizing was a mistake. I can't be helped, but I can clearly be stopped.

And these three are on a mission. Lucky for them, there's so much chaos and lawlessness in Primitus that no one really cares or even notices that I'm being forcibly dragged through the streets. Kicking and clawing, the international sign for abduction, utterly meaningless here. Background noise.

It's as if they somehow know I've closed in on the code, on the secret forbidden knowledge that will awaken humanity, putting an end to their suffering and bringing them into a new higher dimension. One I desperately want to return to, this time with Roman.

But it's sleep that these three feel compelled to preserve, by illusions of separateness spun out of fairy tales of identity. And they want to silence me. And Shamus wants my blood. So their alliance is as natural as the scorching sun that bakes the skin on my shoulders as they lead me up the long walk to the front of the Kings' castle.

Walking through the streets in the King sector is like wading through the disgusting aftermath of fraternity row at the end of rush week. I step over trash, rotting food, and more than a few slumped-over people in outrageous outfits that surely looked better in the dark. Passed out, makeup smeared on their faces, and a fine coat of desert sand caked to their sweating sunburned bodies. Even if I do everything I can to save them, looking around at this hollow existence, at the shallow and weak minded, I know not everyone will make it to the fifth dimension.

Druscilla turns her heavily smoked eyes to me. "Ready to see Shamus?"

"No, not really," I say. "Does that matter?" I ask, hopeful. I am her damn queen after all.

"No, not really." She smiles.

After ascending a mountain of white marble stairs the three of them lead me through a breezy open-air entryway that's as lavish as it is spacious—where everything is white and plush. Then we turn down a long slim corridor; a sandstone tunnel that snakes one way then the next. Winding us ever deeper into the heart of the extravagant castle, until we come to a large iron door, which opens to a well-appointed throne room. The monstrous elaborately carved white ivory chair at the far end the clear focal point, set off by dark fabrics and exotic prints filling the rest of the gargantuan space.

Druscilla cuffs me to a heavy golden pipe that runs along the bottom of the wall at one side of the room, and then walks off with a pompous smirk on her face. The other two are still lurking over me, Bael and Kazaar, and neither is saying a word.

One appears older than the other by the deep creases on his sun-dried face. He gives a gesture toward me.

"Why, thank you, Kazaar," says the younger of the two, Bael. He's the one who dragged me halfway here, as I flung myself around behind him trying to break into flight. When he drops his leg back behind him, I know what's coming. I tense up and close my eyes before his heavy boot slams into my stomach, a swift kick in the gut. Then, Kazaar cuts me with a switch blade.

A few minutes later I'm lying limp on the floor, staring at the big white throne before me. I'm wondering whether Shamus knows he's not my brother, whether finding out will surprise or even hurt him.

Finally, he comes striding slowly toward me across the grand space. His smile grows wider, more maniacal, more frightening with every step.

"Oh Eve..." he laments, sounding strangely intimate, like he's ready to pour his heart out. Then he goes quiet again, continuing his casual stroll.

His greasy blue-black mop of hair has gone ghostly gray. And his once doughy frame is now sunken and gaunt—all the apparent signs of stress from a desperate and ravenous attempt to gain power and then hold on to it.

But it's not power that motivates Shamus. I used to think it was, but I was wrong. He enjoys power a great deal; he always has, but it's not what drives him.

What drives him, always to fantastical levels of destruction, is surprisingly simple. He's driven by life from *his* perspective, by what he imagines has been "done to him," by the illusion he can't break free of, and by the revenge he feels he's due.

An old debt of revenge he's gone to great lengths to settle.

The marble beneath the heels of his expensive-looking shoes creates a thunderous clap that grows louder as he narrows the vast space between us, each deliberate step echoing through me.

Then he stops walking and inhales, sucking what seems like all the air in the cavernous room in through his bulbous nose. I get the feeling he thinks he's discovered how to hold the entire universe in a state of suspended animation with his swollen persona.

"How I *love* to hate you," are the words he finally breathes out, his shoulders and chest dropping, eyes resting on me awash with a look of absolute honesty that I have never seen in them before. I've always known he hates me, of course, but this admission appears to be quite a relief for him, a satisfying release, the incredible pleasure it's given him—the chance to hate me once more.

"I *really* love to hate you," he says. "I *live* for it ... every chance I get."

As he draws closer, closing the last few feet between us, an ancient chill rushes through me.

"And did you know that between love and hate there is very little difference?" he asks, squatting, his face just a foot or two from mine, twisting a strand of my hair around his finger. "Really, it's true. Perhaps even none at all," he explains, like he's telling a riveting tale to a small child. You know who told me that? It was your friend Jude. He said both love and hate bind us in the very same way."

The sarcasm in his voice grows as he continues. "Hate, like love, is merely energy ... pulling us together, time and time and time again. Whether that energy is love or hate is, in fact, completely irrelevant. The energy itself is only weak or strong, but it isn't good or bad; it's neutral," he explains, lecturing me on something I'm not convinced he believes at all. "Yup, everything is neutral. Until, of course, the sordid history of our souls—that rich tapestry of betrayal and hurt, of wounds and revenge—comes along and gives it all meaning. Now how do you suppose that is? That all things are really neutral … cause I can't seem to make heads or tails of it …"

Shamus stares off into a gold-leafed corner of the ceiling. Focusing his gaze beyond the grand fresco of Apollo on a speeding chariot surrounded by winged cherubs, led by Aurora, the goddess of the dawn, he quietly contemplates something. He's always had an uncanny knack for overlooking the truth, staring right past it into black holes, where there's nothing but dead space.

"IS IT TRUE???" he screams, spit flying from his lips. *"You know the truth, don't you?!"* He grabs my cheeks so hard I think he might shatter my teeth.

By the way his face is frozen, waiting, it seems that an answer is required. So despite his vice grip, I shake my head. "No," I lie, as my tears roll over his clenched forefinger and thumb. Tears of physical pain and building rage, but not regret—not a single tear of regret.

Shamus shoves my face from his hand then stands up and straightens his ridiculously opulent clothes. He's unstable, more irrational than I've ever seen before. Only now he's also much more powerful. Now he fires missiles into the sky for fun. He dumps people out of airplanes into the Grand Canyon, both living and dead.

He looms over me. Having the upper hand is so pleasing to him he appears momentarily lost for words, his dark eyes relishing every bit of my hopeless predicament.

"I won't lie to you, beloved sister. Your situation is grim at best."

He is right about that at least.

"Tell us, what's it going to be?" he taunts, as if I have some kind of choice. "Your life or Valeria's? It wouldn't be any kind of *good* life, mind you."

Valeria's death—and that of the child she's carrying, eleven months and counting, the last on Earth—or my death, and subsequently the death of the rest of the human race. Not just figuratively, not just missing our chance to leave this dimension—real death, as he explains.

"Your vial. The Soros. We have scientists here too, you know. It's airborne now. Everyone, save for my beautiful new souls, everyone, from those fools in Rugby to the retched old souls in Antiquus—even Jakob." He grins at me. "So that one you might want to consider. And of course, there's the blood."

I watch, almost fascinated, as it pools around my body. Spilling out in waves and gushes.

My blood.

He starts pacing like a lecturing professor. "Did you

know that there's actually gold in human blood? Don't answer that. I'd be very annoyed if you already knew. Your blood's been kind of a reoccurring theme, hasn't it?"

I haven't really thought about it, but he's right. Ever since Animus arrived in Rugby. From that day on, there has always been something about my blood. It, too, is a riddle. I see that now as it pours out of me, and as I catch a glimpse into Shamus's soul, a man who in this lifetime and in others I've called family, is so focused on my blood. My blood, he believes, can raise the dead.

"Blood that flows out now, spilling everywhere," he says. "Because of your stupid heart, how it continues to beat … its relentless task to sustain life. The one it does enthusiastically now … killing you."

He smiles. "The heart is a funny thing," he says wistfully, and I see where he's heading: Roman. "He's very sick, Eve, very sick. I'm only glad you've arrived in time to say goodbye."

He waltzes over to me, leaning down to whisper, "And I will relish the power to deprive you of the opportunity."

He sits down next to me. "You know, when you first met him, I had a mind to tell you to go for it, you know? It's only love. What could possibly go wrong?" he asks with a smile. "Things might have turned out differently. But we were never close; you barely know me at all."

"You're not even my brother," I say, feeling a sudden relief.

"I know, silly," he says, smiling and shaking his head. "And since we're talking family trees, here's one for you: Cian's not your grandfather. I'm guessing that may sting a bit, but yes, dear Eve, you are the reject you always thought you were. You're an orphan; no one wanted you. And Cian is my *father*, not my grandfather, and nothing whatsoever to you."

Shamus stands and walks across the grand space. My heart fills with fury as I watch him.

"Have you figured it out yet?" he asks, amused. "That your death would have spared everyone this fate …" he feels it necessary to point out, and of course it would have. The reason why Shamus didn't take my life in Eremis is painfully obvious now: my blood. He's taunting my earlier decision, during my darkest hour, not to take my own life.

Maybe he's right. Maybe I should have let death take me when I had the chance. But the truth was, deep down, in some untraceable place, when the window of fate opened briefly and taking my own life was conceivable—as I even appeared to beg and bargain for the end, for *my* end—this minute invisible space, this shadow of a piece of a shred of my soul just stood in the corner, arms crossed, calling my bluff. Because it knew that I had one critical problem.

I had a riddle to solve.

"I'm grateful," I say.

Shamus whirls around. "What's that?" he perks up, coming back toward me. "Come again? I thought I heard you say that you were grateful ... to *me*?" Utterly fascinated.

"I am. My heart is filled with gratitude. My soul thanks yours."

From the look on Shamus's face, my statement worries him. He doesn't understand what I'm saying, and he doesn't know where I'm going with it, and he doesn't like that. He's always fancied himself much smarter than me, and he truly believes I'm his subordinate—a delusion that's long been his undoing.

"You see, if you *had* killed me," I say, "I wouldn't have gotten to break this little code I've been working on."

I think of what I know, the greatest lie ever told and the all-important truth. Staring at him, I let his ego move aside. The bravado that is Shamus, the wrecking ball, the murderer, the power-hungry little man whose perception has built him a reality of pain, one life after the next. I see the wounds branded all over his ego, the sadness, the hurt. And deeper, underneath it all, I see his soul shining out from behind his blackened eyes, the divine spark, stifled and drowning. Wanting desperately to be brought toward the light, toward love and out of the pain.

"I rejected you a very long time ago," I sigh.

TWENTY

— ❈ —

I reach out my hand to him.

"I did what I thought was right," I tell him, summoning all the love that ever existed, words moving through me from someplace else, from some other lifetime. "It didn't have anything to do with you. It was about my own power."

He walks toward me as I speak, his head cocked to one side and a thirst in his eyes like I've never seen before. Then he reaches out. His hand is shaking as it nears mine. When it's close enough, I take a breath and grab onto it, gently. I know that I have to go the extra distance for him, not because he was ever right but because he deserves love. We all do. Divine love is our birthright, to receive it and to give it away despite wrong and right. Divine love dissolves even the oldest wounds.

Still, I never imagined Shamus letting me go, not really.

But it's exactly what he does. The miracle I wouldn't have even hoped for happening right before my eyes. Because Shamus felt unloved. Because he carried the feeling with him into two hundred lives, allowing it to balloon more and more, and he was ready to set it down. He could have healed it himself. He could have dissolved all his own pain with the truth. But that's the thing about truth in this world—it's so damn hard to find. It's so elusive, you can trip over it and then get up and keep walking along, continuing on your search.

He wasn't able to find it himself, very few can. So I brought the truth to Shamus: that he's loved. And when you know your loved it's much easier to love other people, and much harder to hurt them.

And after leaving him a dizzying amount of my blood— just in case it really does wake the dead, as he's heard it will from, you guessed it, Druscilla, Bael, and Kazaar—he lets me leave. He lets me walk out the big iron front door with Val and Roman, who both seem fine so far.

I grab onto Roman the second I see him.

He's here. And he's alive. All my love for him, the cosmic love I'm only just starting to understand and the human love, the decades of love, centuries of love, lost and found and lost again and again and again. I fling my arms around his shoulders and squeeze myself into him, and his

295

heart beats through his chest and into mine.

Shamus even gives us an airplane, one of the bombers he's been using to dump corpses and the dying into the Grand Canyon. And Phoenix and Jude and Val and Roman and I fly off through the fading light of day, heading for Antiquus.

I have a two-step plan—again. Heal the world from the impending virus and then reveal the forbidden knowledge. Both of which require the resources at Antiquus.

A hunch about my blood and the desire to complete my unfinished business are a strong tailwind as I fly the bomber across the desert.

"I can't get over your eyes," Roman whispers to me from the copilot's seat. "They're so bright."

"You should see them in the dark," I say with a smile, hinting about what I look forward to doing with him once all this is over. And feeling a rush of excitement at having come so far and about everything we are about to do. But my happy moment stops dead when I hear Val cough.

Then, "Sorry Roman. You won't get that chance to see her eyes in the dark," a menacing voice booms from behind us.

It's Kazaar I see as I turn. He's holding Jude by the back of his collar, lifting him like a doll, the way Bael did to me.

"If you look out your window, on the left side of the plane and on the right side of the plane and everywhere underneath, you'll notice the Grand Canyon," he says, like the pilot on the intercom. Then he mashes a large button against the wall near him, and the cargo door begins to drop.

"You think you're the only one with power," he says to me. "I find that so incredibly irritating. I have power. And I've had it a lot longer than you. It's harder to handle then you think, princess."

I motion for Roman to take the controls as I stand up to face him. "Beyond just being on the wrong side of history, you're wrong about a few things." I walk toward him, unrelenting in my stare, feeling invincible. *Knowing* I am.

"The first thing you notice about power, when you truly own it, is that you don't have to tell anyone you have it," I say. "They know. Power is funny that way. And when you see people demanding it, looking to others to give it to them, or trying to prove to themselves and the world how much they have, you just shake your head and walk on. That isn't how power works. It doesn't have to be authenticated, approved, bestowed, or endorsed. Power doesn't need to be created, and it can't be destroyed either. Espousing your own power... that is the very definition of weakness."

Now I'm just a few feet from where Kazaar holds Jude by the edge of the open bomb bay doors, surveying all my options. "True power can't be ignored, so it isn't worth mentioning." I know that Kazaar will gladly give his life to stop me, that his only goal is to get both Jude and me out of this plane.

"And the second major thing you're wrong about is that I am not a princess." I shake my head. "I'm your fucking queen."

I grab a parachute hanging from the wall and dive into him. The three of us tumble toward the earth, toward mountains of dead bodies below, Kazaar and I both locked onto Jude.

Kazaar is screaming, and his eyes are wild and unfocused. There is no fear at all in Jude when his steady gaze meets mine, even as we blaze downward like rockets headed for the earth. I have no fear at all either. I'm not afraid to die, but I want to stay alive—there's a big difference.

Jude spots a carabineer, and in the blink of an eye, he clips it to his belt loop and to mine. I grab Jude's hand, feeling the rush of power that flows between us. We agree silently to open the parachute in three, two, one …

Jude grabs the string and rips the parachute from the pack. We sail upward, hanging onto each other and watching the terror on Kazaar's face as he falls toward the heap of dead humanity.

Realizing that I don't know whether Roman can land an airplane, much less a bomber in the Grand Canyon, I try something. It's the only thing I've got right now. I close my eyes and tell Roman, telepathically, to radio to Rugby, to Seth, who will be Roman's best chance of talking him down to the ground, just like he talked me off a ledge.

Seth is good like that. He has no trouble guiding Roman through the landing, quipping that he isn't offended that Roman has done remotely what took Seth years to learn, because, "Roman's freakishly high IQ is going to make it hard for him to have any real friends."

Then he does us one more little favor.

"Done," he says from his new hacker heaven in Rugby headquarters. He's killed all the power to Antiquus, including the elaborate network of backup generators.

I've already woken the sleeping dragon. Now it's time to slay it.

TWENTY-ONE

——— ❈ ———

Antiquus is a dizzying place with the lights on. Far too big for its own good, labyrinths within labyrinths. So with the unending corridors and winding passages all unlit, it will be the stuff nightmares are made of. Fortunately, I can see perfectly in the dark now, somehow more clearly than in the light. Jude and I both can. And that will be our greatest advantage.

From the moment I tell them the plan, Roman and Phoenix both hate it.

"No way. Forget it," Roman objects.

They strongly disagree, coming up with alternate ideas, debating me. And when that doesn't work, they whine and protest. But I don't care. I know what I have to do. And I know how to do it. I've been preparing for this for a very long time.

After we leave Roman and Phoenix in my room to watch over Val, Jude and I run to the biotech tower. It is alarming to not see anyone at all as we dash from my room deep beneath the earth to the Foundation, past the Subterranean, and into the Towers. But I am just worried about the first task at hand.

Looking at my own blood under a microscope.

"I knew it!" I declare, then scoot over to let Jude have a look. On one side of the slide is my blood, on the other, the Soros virus. One glance and I see how they fit together, and so does Jude. I see the antibodies clear as day, like red floating keys to the locks of the genetic structure of the virus.

Within five minutes, I've made an antidote. I will inject Val first, who'd begun to cough on the plane and is now running a fever of one hundred two. I'm able to detect her exact body temperature just by looking at her, and I can see the virus in her cough.

I'm starting to suspect that Roman is somehow immune, that he and I and Jude and Phoenix all are. That aside from our birthdays and a critical role in the "apocalypse," this is another thing we have in common—but it's just a hunch.

When Jude and I return to my room, Phoenix lets us in. Val looks awful.

"Her fever must have spiked or something, I don't know," Phoenix speculates off Val's chattering teeth and incessant sweating as she paces around the bed like a caged tiger. She would much rather drive a stake through someone's chest to protect Val than sit by her bed and hold her hand as she moans.

I don't even have to say that her fever is now 104.2 before Jude is bringing cold water and a small towel from my bathroom. I dunk the towel, wring it, and gently place it on Val's forehead.

"Where's Roman," I ask, suddenly realizing that he's not here doing what I'm doing, trying to cool Val's fever.

Phoenix doesn't answer.

"What?" I demand, and at the same time beg her not to say what I'm thinking.

"He went to find Jakob. He's going to kill him."

"Shit!" I yell, so loud it jars Val awake.

"Sorry," I say, placing my hands on her round belly, feeling the baby move, a rolling wave of elbows and heels pressing against Val's hot feverish skin.

"I couldn't stop him," Phoenix says.

Now it's my turn not to answer, a hand still pressed on Val's belly, knowing that Phoenix could have stopped Roman if she wanted to. What is it about these damn two-step plans?

After dosing Val with the antidote, cringing at making her wince as I sink the needle into her arm, Jude and I take off. Leaving Phoenix "trapped like a rat," as she put it. Having to play Florence Nightingale during the final epic battle must be driving her practically mad. But Val needs protecting, and I figure that maybe it will hasten Phoenix's enlightenment, as acute suffering has a potent way of doing.

It's time for the second step of the plan. The truth has been decoded, and now we have to get the message to as many people as possible, whether they believe it or not. Whether they can awaken from the illusion, that will be up to them.

"You go to the technology tower," I tell Jude. "Figure out how to power up the closed-circuit monitors, sync up with Rugby and Primitus, and wait there." I take off toward where I know I'll find Roman—in his room, where I left the ax.

Roman had asked me on the plane what I'd done with it. And casually enough that I told him without thinking. Sometimes his smolder was like scopolamine in the water— his chiseled face had a way of turning me into a zombie.

As I dash toward Roman's tower, something stops me dead in my tracks. Something I see out of the corner of my eye. I back up and look out the little window I've just run past to see Roman and Jakob wrestling over my ax in the middle of a glass walkway between two towers, a thousand feet above the ground.

I hear a crackling sound out of a nearby speaker, then a whirling as power rushes to the closed-circuit monitors, all of them kicking on at once. And then Jude's voice echoes throughout the empty halls and stairways.

"Eve, I'm going to start. It's time."

I look out the window at the full moon hanging high above the struggle between Roman and Jakob. It's huge, round, and glowing orange, and it flickers in and out. I stare at it, knowing that either this reality is dissolving into something new, or the time for ascent is rapidly coming to a close. Jude is about to begin revealing the truth, the forbidden knowledge that will end this world for good.

I have already told Jude the entire code. He knows as much as I do now. After what happened with Kazaar on the plane, I told him everything. In case one of us didn't make it, the hidden truth could be revealed no matter what.

"They tell you that you're separate," Jude announces, "they tell you you're divided, they teach this to you from the time you're very young ..."

My eyes on Roman, something terrifying occurs to me, something that shakes my soul and nearly shatters it into a billion pieces—that Roman can't hear any of this. I watch them through the window, struggling for their lives over the ax, and I know there is no way he's hearing what Jude is saying. There are no speakers in the glass walkways. The speakers are everywhere throughout Antiquus, everywhere but in the clear glass tunnels running from one tower to the next.

I told Jude *and not Roman*, I realize, my stomach plummeting.

What was I thinking? How had I done that? Why hadn't I thought to tell him? Had my soul chosen to go to the fifth dimension with Jude over Roman? The thought of it sends a blaze of fear through me. I race toward the entrance to the glass walkway where Roman and Jakob are struggling.

"The truth is," Jude goes on, "that we're fully connected to the source of all life. We are momentary tendrils of this source with which we are one. But here in this dimension, *perception* has been shaping reality. And through the creation of different perceptions comes a feeling of separateness, from our source and from one another. Perception is one of two things we've been sent here to learn about. Power is the other. These two lessons, power and perception, are easily interwoven, working in symbiotic perfection through the continuous manipulation of manufactured identities. Things such as race, belief systems, nationality, culture, economic status, none of which was ever the truth of who you are. None of which was ever you. Remember? How it all dissolves away when we leave this world? The color of our skin, where on the globe we lived, whether we were rich or poor, an old soul or new, only fabrications meant to shape a perspective temporarily placed into our minds, to experience varying degrees of power, none of which was ever real. And an even bigger lie is holding all of it in place … the greatest lie ever told."

As I run through the passageways of Antiquus, Roman not hearing what Jude's saying, missing the secret forbidden knowledge—it's too much to bear.

I round the last corner to the entrance to the tunnel. At some point during their brutal fight, the ax had been kicked away, or thrown, and now it lays by my feet. Jakob has Roman's neck in his hands, choking him and banging his head against the glass with all his strength. I pick up the ax and advance on them like a dark tide washing through the glass tunnel, the iron beast resting and ready on my shoulder. As I close in, Jakob's eyes flick up, and he jumps off Roman, sliding backward, away from me and my ax, terrified.

Roman sits up, choking and gasping for air.

"Let's go, Roman. Come on!" I yell. "Please, you have to hear something!"

Roman stands and looks at me, mystified. All I see is his

rage for Jakob. It's like a drug. It's the only thing in the entire world he can feel or focus on.

"Let's just go," I beg him. "It doesn't matter now."

"It doesn't *matter*?" he asks in disbelief. "It matters, Eve, because of how much you matter to me."

"Roman, he can't hurt me," I say, fearing that it's impossible to reach someone lost so deeply in rage.

"He *did* hurt you. And I have to hurt him as much as he's hurt us." He rips the ax from my hands and barrels down on Jakob, who braces himself for the attack.

Roman cocks the ax over his shoulder like a baseball bat and swings it in a brutal uppercut. The blade lands square on the side of Jakob's head, and his body explodes into a billion shards of black matter, first hanging in the air where he stands, then suddenly sucked away through the other end of the tunnel.

Then Jude's words are all around me; I'm hearing them without a speaker. Watching Roman, his back to me, how he's standing so still, he seems to be listening.

"Why do you think Eve was not supposed to eat the apple from the tree of the knowledge of good and evil? If we really thought about that, if we looked at it differently than we were taught to look at it, then we'd see the instructions encoded: eat the apple, Eve, eat the apple and know the truth. The forbidden fruit of the tree of knowledge of good and evil is the truth that there is no good and evil. But in Eve, we had someone to blame. The woman, she was weak, shameful, a bad influence—even evil. So the story goes. Setting in stone the lessons at work in this world, a perfectly created *perception* for lessons of *power*. It started with Eve, and it's worked very well for a very long time. That's why we weren't to eat of it, why we were told in every generation and in every language, because if we knew the secret, the knowledge that there is no good and evil, we'd no longer be locked in that struggle. And when you disengage with any struggle, it simply dissolves. The lie of good and evil is the greatest lie ever told. The all-important truth is that your perceptions are a myth, and all the power in the universe already resides within us and always has."

After Jude's final words, Roman turns to me. His face and body and clothes are covered in blood, Jakob dead at his feet, a mix of shock and relief—and vindication, that the evil is destroyed. That's when I know.

It's too late ... *for Roman.*

And as I feel myself melting from this dimension into the next—trying to keep him in my sight as long as possible, I finally realize. This life is so full of poetry— Cian's nightstand, and whatever's in it, was never for me. The key that Jude had worn around his neck was always meant to end up in the hands of *my* soul mate. He'd been holding it for Roman the whole time.

"We're all connected," I marvel. "Don't you see?" I lift the key over my neck. Roman begins slowly walking toward me, his face awash in confusion.

"What's happening?" he asks, staring at me, frowning, the gore-spattered ax still hanging from his hand.

I can only imagine how I must look to him. I'm no longer seeing the same world he's seeing. The air shimmers from light particles reflected by the moon, the glass pixelating all around us—the walkway that doesn't really exist.

"There are beings all around you," I tell Roman as I stare at his army of guides. "Light beings, angels, and archangels ..." I try describing these ascended heavenly creatures to him, but Roman can't listen; his worst fear is coming true.

"They're here to help you," I say. "Talk to them and learn to hear them. Let them guide you. Roman, there will be suffering."

"Eve, why are you telling me this?" he stammers, his breath heavy.

"It's going to be okay," I say.

"No!" He runs toward me, reaching out. "Don't go! Don't go, Eve!"

From the sheer terror on his face, I know I'm disappearing

before him, and because he's disappearing before me.

"How will I find you?" He stops short before reaching me, his eyes searching.

I throw the key and watch him catch it.

Then he's gone.

End of Book Two

ACKNOWLEDGEMENTS

Good people had to suffer terribly for this story to go from a spark in my mind into a book. As you might imagine those who spin tales about the whole world being an illusion, who believe nothing is what it seems, and who generally get very little sleep, can be rather intense to be around. It takes a very special person to really love them and an even more rare soul to help them creatively.

I'll start with my youngest daughter. Quinn, I'm sorry I mentioned the thing about the moon not being real, that may have been one too many conspiracies for your twelve year old brain to digest on your morning car ride to school. Thank you for always following me down the rabbit hole— and rest easy, I'm *pretty* sure the moon is real.

To my oldest, Kade, thank you for straight up refusing to read any of my books to this day, even though your friends have. Enduring a mother who writes about teenage love just as you enter high school, in retrospect, probably sucks. I hope you continue to choose me over my books.

Tela Kayne, I'm sure other moms talk about their kids and stuff when they take walks with friends, which is why we always lower our voices when we pass someone while in the midst of discussing sacred geometry, or Fibonacci number sequences. I only hope unraveling the mysteries of the universe and solving all the world's problems in under an hour is as fun for you as it is for me, and if not, thanks for pretending so well that it is.

And Don, my blessing of a husband who loves me impossible amounts, here was my plan. When you reached your breaking point, shouldering all the grown-up responsibilities of our life while I played make believe all day, when I sensed you were just about to snap, I'd reveal that I based Roman on you and make it all better. *Don, I based Roman on you.*

ABOUT THE AUTHOR

Tiffany has said that the story of The Oldest Soul had been "making its presence known" for several years.

Eve first sprang into her mind—like a bucket of cold water in the face—while on a walk in 2011, she promptly went home and wrote the first 4 pages (which have remained unchanged since). But she filed Eve's one-of-a–kind journey away in her mind when work on other projects beckoned.

"I've been a writer of all forms of stories since I was around seventeen and the success of a couple of my TV pilots took me further from Eve's story, but what I didn't realize was that I was always amassing inspiration for what would one day become *The Oldest Soul*. Everything in my world somehow always circled back to Eve."

In the spring and summer of 2015, in a matter of months, she breathed life into ANIMUS, or rather, it breathed life into her … "The story is a force of nature—and seemed to move through me like an incredible breath of life from someplace else."

Tiffany has always said that stories "know what they want to be." And that as a writer she feels it's her job to "show up and get out of the way." Never has that felt so true than when Eve is telling her story.

"Elaborate worlds infused with real human emotions and strong characters with thought provoking stories are what fill my soul." Tiffany has spent the past few years creating such worlds in the form of original feature screenplays and TV pilots as a screenwriter. She lives outside of Atlanta with her husband, their two beautiful daughters and Chloe — the best dog in the world!